The Kindling

Read the other exciting books in the
Fire-us Trilogy
coming soon!

BOOK 2: THE KEEPERS OF THE FLAME

BOOK 3: THE KILN

TRILOGY: BOOK 1

JENNIFER ARMSTRONG AND NANCY BUTCHER

HarperCollins*Publishers*

Library of Congress Cataloging-in-Publication Data
Armstrong, Jennifer.
   The kindling / Jennifer Armstrong and Nancy Butcher.
      p.   cm.—(Fire-us trilogy ; Book 1)
   Summary: In 2007, a small band of children have joined together in a Florida
town, trying to survive in a world where it seems that all the adults have been
killed off by a catastrophic virus.
   ISBN 0-06-008048-5 — ISBN 0-06-029411-6 (lib. bdg.)
   [1. Survival—Fiction. 2. Science fiction.] I. Butcher, Nancy. II. Title.
PZ7.A73366 Ki 2002   2001039679
[Fic]—dc21   CIP
                                                                        AC

1 2 3 4 5 6 7 8 9 10
❖
First Edition

For Anne Ginkel
—J.A.

For Jens David Ohlin
—N.B.

When Fire-us came in summertime 2002, First Mommies and First Daddies tried to run away from it. They put us in the cars and we left our First Homes. But then Fire-us caught them and they burnt up, and us kids were left alone here in the hot place. We lost our names. We lost our brothers and sisters. We can't remember who we were. But now we're Teacher and Mommy and Hunter, and we have little ones with us. We're a family.

—*The Book, page 1*

Chapter One

Teacher sat at her desk in the pink-flower bedroom, working on the lesson for tomorrow's class. As the oldest kid in the family, it was her job to teach the little ones, to make sure they didn't run around like wild animals. But nobody had ever told her how to be a teacher. She had to make it up as she went. Now she was hunched over The Book, searching for inspiration. She had been stuck on page 14 for a while:

> TAURUSES: 2002 IS YOUR YEAR! AS NEPTUNE GOES INTO RETROGRADE, YOU WILL FIND INCREDIBLE OPPORTUNITIES FOR CHANGE, PERSONAL GROWTH—AND ROMANCE!

EASY ON SINKS. TOUGH ON GERMS.

IMPORTANT SAFETY INSTRUCTIONS:
When using your telephone unit, these simple safety precautions should always be observed in order to lessen the risk of electrical shock, fire, and injury.

STRONG ENOUGH FOR A MAN.
CLEARLY MADE FOR YOU.

DANGER! CUIDADO!

Teacher picked up a pen and wrote on a blank piece of paper: *Tauruses, telephones*. And then she crossed out those words and wrote, below them: *2002, germs, fire, man, danger*. She swung her feet under her chair, banging against the rungs. The words blurred together in her vision for a moment.

With a sharp swipe of her pen, she crossed those words out, too. Teacher shook her head, and then turned her attention back to The Book. She began turning the pages slowly, gingerly. Some of the clippings and photographs she'd pasted in over the last five years were starting to peel away; they crackled as she turned the pages. She made a mental note to herself to take care of that one of these days. She should send Hunter for more glue or paste—whatever he could find.

A passage on page 104, written in purple ink, caught her attention:

A DREAM

We are at a picnic in the park. There are people everywhere—Grown-ups, children, babies. And dogs running around. But where is our dog? He must have gone off again, probably chasing a Frisbee somewhere.

First Daddy is making hot dogs on the grill. First Mommy is helping him; they're laughing about something. I look up at them: they're big tall Grown-ups. There is a little girl with us—who is she? Curly blond hair. She's wearing a pink tutu over her T-shirt and shorts. She keeps begging *me to play catch with her.*

*I finally say yes, and she hugs me. She won't
let go. "Let's play catch, okay? Stop hugging
me." But she still won't let go.*

Teacher trailed her fingers down the page. The purple words were in her handwriting. The thing was, she didn't remember writing them, couldn't even remember whose dream it was. This was starting to happen more and more often with The Book—these unfamiliar entries. Often she woke up in the mornings, slumped at her desk, The Book still open under her cheek.

A branch tapped at the window. Traffic on the street. Sprinklers hissing and a radio chattering from next door, a vacuum cleaner droning, the hum of an air conditioner—sometimes these sounds seemed so real. *So real.* As if they were really out there, along with Grown-ups and pets and report cards and soccer games.

Teacher closed her eyes and made herself listen to the sounds she really *could* hear. Downstairs: that was Mommy puttering around the kitchen, cupboard doors banging and shutting. A humid breeze wafted through the open window, carrying with it the sounds of Baby and Doll playing their silly dolly games. "Yes, eat all your beets, all your beets like a good dolly," came the singsong voices.

Teacher wondered if Teddy Bear was with them. He was always so quiet, half the time you had no idea if he was around. Action Figure was probably off someplace, maybe with Hunter. She hoped they came home soon. It was going to storm. She could smell the dampness in the air that lay on her skin like extra clothes.

She opened her eyes and blinked. She stared at the thing above her desk, the thing she had never liked but had never thought to take down: a painting of a girl riding a horse. It lay against the faded cream wallpaper with the tiny pink roses and the blooming stains of mildew.

Teacher often wondered about the person who had put it there, the person who had lived in this room in the Before Time, before Fire-us. Had the person been a girl? The girl on the horse, even? Were they the same age? And was that girl even alive anymore?

Mommy's voice cut into her thoughts: *"Girrr-rrls! Dinner! Come in and wash your hands!"*

Teacher sighed. The lessons for tomorrow's class would have to wait until later. It was best to work late at night, anyway, after everyone had gone to bed. There was total silence then, except for the twanging of bullfrogs and the occasional scream of a panther. Once in a while the little kids might cry or babble in their sleep, but that was a good thing—that was Information.

"Dinner!" Mommy yelled again.

Teacher started to close The Book, and then hesitated. It was open to page 128—when had she turned to that page? Bright red words leaped out at her:

LOSE 15 POUNDS IN 15 DAYS WITH THE AMAZING NEW PASTA AND PAPAYA DIET!

Teacher frowned. A vague, troubling thought niggled

at her. Food. Something about food. Something bad.

The answer must be in The Book, if only she knew what to look for. She bent her head over the stiff and rippled pages and turned them one by one. Being a teacher was a hard job. She would skip dinner. She wasn't hungry anyway.

Mommy opened the cabinet over the sink, standing on tiptoe to see to the back. The two little girls came in through the screen door.

"I want Cereos for dinner, Mommy!" Baby said.

"Cereos, Cereos," Doll chanted. She propped her dolly up on the table and danced it from side to side as she sang. Its one blinky eye batted open and shut.

Teddy Bear bent his head over his addition worksheet, scooting his chair closer under the table. Late afternoon light slanting through the vine-covered window turned his paper as green as swamp water.

"We're out of Cereos. How about applesauce?"

"Again?" wailed Doll.

Mommy boosted herself up onto the counter to examine the shelves more closely. There wasn't much left. She'd have to make a long shopping list. First Mommy had always made a shopping list.

"You can have applesauce or beets."

Baby made a face. "No! No beets!"

The window over the sink slid open, and a second boy crawled through, throwing his knapsack onto the floor. "Want ice cream!"

The children at the table stared at him, their mouths open. On the counter, Mommy was very still. Her heart was pounding: it always did that whenever she was reminded of something special from the Before Time. A fly zzzzzed against the screen door. After a moment, Baby let out a wail that echoed in the kitchen.

"There's no such thing as ice cream, is there, Mommy? Isn't that just a made-up thing? Isn't it?"

Mommy jumped down off the counter. She bent to pick up the knapsack and examined the boy's face for dirt. He was filthy.

"We used to have ice cream in the Before Time," she replied. She made herself sound matter-of-fact. "We just don't have it anymore. Wash your face, Action. How did you get so dirty?"

"Lookit I got," Action Figure said, grabbing the knapsack from her hand. He unclipped the flap and spilled a dozen oranges out onto the table. The other children lunged at them, ripping them open and eating the fruit out of the skins.

"Mmm, mmm, good," Teddy Bear sang, wiping juice from his chin.

Doll pretended to feed some orange to her dolly. "Eat it all up or no bessert!"

Mommy dipped a washcloth into a bucket of clean rainwater in the sink and began scrubbing at Action Figure's grimy face. That's what mommies were supposed to do. The boy struggled in her grip and let out a low growl.

"No!" Mommy held his chin. "Stop that." She finished scrubbing his face and tossed the washcloth back into the sink. She wanted to check his scalp for ticks, but she would have to wait until he was sleepy and less likely to bite.

Baby crawled across the table, smearing juice, and

eyed Teddy Bear's addition worksheet. He tried to snatch it away from her, but she held it up and waved it in the air. The bow on her grubby lace baby bonnet waved under her chin as she jiggled up and down.

"Mommy, Teddy isn't doing his homework. He's doing alligator pictures again."

Mommy took the worksheet. Among the columns of numbers that Teacher had written down for Teddy Bear to add, he had drawn alligators in different poses. Some crawled among the sums, some dragged babies down staircases of numbers, some were half submerged in murky water. Teddy Bear stared up at Mommy with wide eyes.

"We talked about this, Teddy," Mommy said. "They don't come into the house. You're safe here."

Doll held her dolly in front of her face. Her voice came out muffled as she spoke through the doll's matted hair. "Dolly saw a alginator yesterday. It was eating a—"

Mommy grabbed the toy away from Doll's face. "Your dolly *did not* see an alligator."

Teddy Bear began crying. Tears made damp half circles under his eyes. He dragged up the hem of his T-shirt and wiped his face on the stained and faded picture of a cartoon mouse. The name of the mouse was The Mouse. At least that was what they thought. They couldn't really remember.

Mommy gave Teddy Bear a hug and helped him wipe his nose on his shirt. Doll scrambled off her chair and threw her arms around Teddy Bear, too.

"I'm sorry, Teddy. Dolly was lying. She didn't see a allingator."

"Action," Mommy said over Teddy Bear's head, "go

check the yard. See if there are any gators there. If not, I think you should all go out and get some fresh air before bedtime. You all had enough oranges, didn't you? Did you leave some for Teacher and Hunter?"

"Yes, Mommy," Baby said.

Action Figure plucked a walkie-talkie off his belt, dashed across the kitchen, and opened the screen door with a judo kick. It swung open and slapped against the wall as he burst into the carport. He held the walkie-talkie to his mouth and made a crackling noise in his throat.

"Okay!" he shouted. "Gator free! Over!"

One by one, the kids trooped past Mommy and out the door. Mommy watched them through the screen as they melted into the late-afternoon dimness of the backyard. Huge tufts of pampas grass rose in hillocks among the vine-tangled palmettos. Gray strings of Spanish moss hung from the live oak that towered over one corner, leaning against the chain-link fence and bowing it outward. The pool, filled with garbage and stagnant water, shimmered greenly as a breeze stirred the surface. A storm was coming. She hoped Hunter would get back before the rain started.

Mommy stood in the doorway, listening to the high-pitched cries and shouts of the children. A cloud of midges hovered in the air in front of her; through them she saw the pale gray of Action Figure's T-shirt as he swarmed up and over the fence. He was probably going to the playground at the elementary school down the street. She had a cloudy memory of the slide, and the jungle gym, and the ropes course from the last time she was out of the house.

But that was back in the Fire-us year, 2002—almost five years ago. Was it that long? Back when she was only nine.

Hunter tied double knots in the laces of his new sneakers, keeping an eye on the gull that strutted across the floor of the shoe store, pecking at leaf scraps and flicking them away. Gulls could get nasty sometimes. Hunter threw one of his old sneakers at the bird, and it flapped away through the broken shop window, squawking. Hunter grabbed his knapsack and stuffed two pairs of size 1s in for the little girls and then hitched it over his shoulder and headed out. As he passed the counter, a gust of wind set the packages of shoelaces on a rack swaying.

Even now, the burned smell from the bookstore next door was strong. Something about the humidity seemed to make the charred shop stink more on some days than others. Out on the street, Hunter walked past vine-covered cars without a glance. He had long since picked them all clean. They had once been filled with useful things: pens and pencils and electronic calculators in purses and briefcases, bags of groceries, suitcases stuffed with clothes. There had been plenty of money, but after the fun of carrying wads of cash wore off, there was no point in hunting it.

Hunter was proud of his hunting. He only brought home useful things, things they needed. His job was important, and he was an important part of the family. Even though he was younger than Teacher, he could do Grown-up things, too.

Fat clouds swelled on the horizon, over the tops of palm trees and magnolias, and a wet wind stirred the branches. Three white pelicans oared themselves through the yellow-gray air. Hunter followed them with his eyes, wishing he could see better. Then another movement caught his attention. He turned, squinting down the street.

"Action?" he called out. "That you?"

Nobody answered. Branches stirred overhead again. Hunter kicked an arm bone out of his path and continued down the sidewalk. Winn-Dixie, over there at at the end of the block, didn't have much left, but he thought he remembered some cartons of powdered milk in the stockroom he hadn't opened yet. As long as the boxes hadn't gotten damp, it'd be okay. Milk would be nice. Mommy was always asking him to hunt more milk. And he could pick up some more batteries if he could find some that still had a charge. Even with their solitary little family as the only shoppers, the town of Lazarus was running out of things to hunt.

Saplings and tall grasses waved among the cracks in the pavement at the supermarket. The parking lot was littered with rusted heaps of shopping carts. All the windows had been broken out of the big market. Hunter just hoisted himself over the sill and into the store, stepping into a shallow puddle that stretched back into the darkness. He fumbled a flashlight out of his knapsack and switched it on.

The smell was usually the worst thing. Animals had made their homes in the supermarkets, gnawing on boxes and bags. Their droppings coated the floors. It was a lucky thing that even sharp teeth couldn't get through cans or jars or else the kids would have starved long ago. The beam of Hunter's flashlight caught red eyes that winked away. His new sneakers crunched over broken glass, and from somewhere at the front of the store came an answering crackle.

Hunter froze halfway down the detergent aisle. He knew his eyes weren't so good, but his hearing was perfect. Someone else was in the Winn-Dixie with him, and it wasn't just a rat. There was a soft splashing sound, a footstep on the wet floor. Hunter's heart thudded in his chest, but he whispered to himself: *Be a man.*

Out loud, he yelled, "Who is it? I know you're there!"

Rustlings and scurryings came from all sides, but no voice replied. Hunter turned around and strode back toward the front of the store, slicing his flashlight beam back and forth in broad sweeps. The ruins of the market lay in heaps and dark, sticky stains. Shards of glass twinkled in the light. Up front, beyond the broken windows, the darkening sky boiled with thunderclouds. Lightning flared, and the broad puddle reflected the flash. Hunter heard a small whimper, like a cat mewing.

Just a cat, he told himself, beginning to head back to the stockroom again. But then he thought—maybe the girls would like a pet. Teacher probably wouldn't let them keep it, but Mommy might say it was okay. He'd find the cat and take it back with him as a surprise. On the other hand, there weren't many cats left. Mostly they got picked off by the big predators. There could be one, though.

Stealthily, he began peering between the checkout lanes. From the two 10-items-or-less lanes he made his way, one cash register at a time, down the row. Lightning flashed again and was answered with a boom of thunder.

At the last lane he ducked and peered under the cash register, arcing his flashlight beam into the dark cubby.

Behind him was a scrabbling sound. Hunter lunged up but banged his head on the underside of the cash register drawer. Cursing, he hauled himself upright. As lightning flashed again, he thought he saw two little figures jumping out the broken front windows. But the light was gone, leaving him dazzled, and he couldn't be sure what he had seen.

Because there were no other children in Lazarus, Florida. As far as Hunter knew, he and Teacher and Mommy, Action Figure, Baby, Doll, and Teddy Bear were the only people left alive in the whole world.

Chapter Two

Hunter sprinted to the broken front window and peered out. Darkness. Lightning flashed in the mud-black sky, and for a moment the parking lot was illuminated. In that brief, photographic second he saw—or thought he saw— two small figures, the same two small figures, darting behind an old aqua station wagon. And then it was the mud-black darkness again.

Children, they're children, they're children, he thought.

He ran out of the Winn-Dixie, using the front entrance this time, like a real customer. The doors were stuck permanently open, ever since the Year of Fire-us when all the electricity had gone, disappeared, died. He ran through the parking lot, only partly aware of the fat, wet drops that pelted his face and the dusty, steamy smell that rose from the asphalt pavement.

The aqua station wagon was one of a dozen cars in the parking lot. An enormous gray pelican was sitting on top of it, preening its feathers in the rain.

Hunter slowed his steps, crouched down, and began circling the vehicle. There was no one, nothing, near or behind or under it. He pointed the beam of his flashlight through the broken windows. A gold cross hanging from the rearview mirror, a Happy Meal bag in the front seat. A skeleton dressed in jeans and sneakers and a faded denim shirt.

Hunter cursed. He had missed that one; he would have to come back for it later and dispose of it. He continued circling, then moved on to another nearby vehicle, a red convertible with a bumper sticker that read MOTHER-IN-LAW IN TRUNK. The convertible was small, open, nowhere for the two creatures to hide. Some birds had made a nest in the front seat long ago. There was a dirty tangle of branches and feathers, gray-white droppings, slivers of pale blue eggshell, and one unopened unborn egg.

Hunter made his way through the rest of the parking lot. It was raining in earnest now, terrible sheets of it like an assault. *Where are they?* he wondered, sipping rain off his lips.

A gust of wind, and a piece of paper flew up and plastered his face. It smelled a bit like pee. He peeled it off in disgust. It was an old, handwritten ad, FREE PUPPIES AND KITTENS TO GOOD HOMES!

It was time to give up. He could try again tomorrow morning, when it wasn't raining. When it would be easier—a little easier—to see.

Running home down the road, his new sneakers slopping through puddles, his pack with no food in it slapping against his back, Hunter thought: *Maybe I was wrong, made a mistake. Maybe they were wild dogs or raccoons or even ghosts.* Teacher read to the children about ghosts sometimes, during School, and Hunter knew by the way she read the stories that she believed in them. Something in her voice. Hunter sort of believed in them, too. He often saw things, shadowy apparition-like things. He saw them in the windows of the abandoned homes, in the palmetto groves, in the old cemetery next to the Buena Vista Estates.

Their house swam into view: white stucco with the orange tiles on the roof and a yellowing palm tree, the humped mass of oleanders that crowded the driveway, the banyan tree spreading in the yard. He slowed his steps and rubbed his eyes, rubbed the rain and tiredness out of them. It was such work, this seeing. His stomach grumbled, and he realized that he hadn't eaten since breakfast.

Inside, Mommy and Teacher were sitting across from each other at the kitchen table. Hunter set his pack down on the counter. He realized that his clothes were soaked and clinging to his skin, that he was dripping all over the linoleum floor. He also realized, with a pang, that his brand-new, just-hunted white sneakers were completely covered with mud.

"You missed dinner," Mommy said. Her eyes were bloodshot: she'd been crying?

From upstairs, Hunter could hear the sounds of Baby and Doll and Teddy Bear playing. "A-lli-gators all around," came Baby's singsong voice.

"Stop it, stop it, stop it," came Teddy Bear's answering wail.

"Anything left?" Hunter asked Mommy.

Mommy sucked in a quick breath and shook her head, making her brown curls flop back and forth. "No, no oranges. The children finished them off. But there's some beets and applesauce."

"You said that was for tomorrow," Teacher said to Mommy. An accusation.

"So Hunter doesn't get to eat? Is that what you mean?" Mommy replied, startled.

Hunter debated for a second. "It's okay. I'm not that

hungry anyway," he lied.

Teacher gazed at his pack, which lay on the counter in a growing pool of rainwater. "What did you bring us?"

"No food," Hunter admitted. "But I got shoes for the girls. And vitamins."

"Shoes!" Teacher slammed her thin sun-browned hand on the table. "Shoes! We don't need shoes, we need food!"

"Teacher," Mommy said.

"I was going to get food," Hunter explained. "I was in the Winn-Dixie. But then I—I thought I saw something."

"Saw something? Saw what?" Teacher asked. She cocked her head and frowned.

Hunter hesitated, staring at the floor. "I saw two—creatures. Children. Maybe." He heard Mommy gasp, and added, "But I don't know."

Mommy was shaking her head in amazement. "Children!"

"I don't know," Hunter repeated. "Might have been dogs. It was dark. It was hard to see."

Teacher got up abruptly from her chair and began pacing around the kitchen. "Children, dogs, whatever. How tall were they?" she demanded.

Hunter thought for a second, then raised his hand in the air to indicate. A few inches shorter than Baby and Doll.

"Were they wearing clothes?" Teacher asked.

"It was dark!" Hunter cried out. He didn't want to tell her about his eyesight, how bad it was. He wasn't sure if everyone had trouble seeing things clearly or if it was just him.

Another sound from upstairs: Action Figure doing his nightly target practice. *"Bam-bam-bam-bam-bam-bam!"* came the staccato sound of his voice.

Mommy stood up, grabbing the edge of the table as she did so. "If there are kids out there, we have to find them," she announced. "We have to take care of them."

"But we *can't* take care of them!" Teacher shouted. "How can we feed more kids? According to The Book we're about to enter a Time of Famine. Did you not admit to me just minutes ago that we don't have enough food to feed our own family? That if Hunter doesn't have a successful hunting expedition soon, we'll run out of food in two, three days, tops?"

Hearing this, Hunter sank to the floor, squatted, covered his eyes with his wet, mud-covered hands. "It wasn't kids!" he whispered. "It couldn't be kids!"

Teacher opened her eyes. Pale gray light shone through the windows, through the filmy white curtains of her room.

Morning.

She rubbed her eyes and glanced around. She was sitting up in her bed, propped up against two pillows. She was still dressed in the same too-small, musty-smelling sundress from yesterday—the one with the daisies on it that Hunter had hunted for her during the First Year from a neighbor's house.

She yawned and stretched. Her muscles were achy tired.

She didn't remember falling asleep. She had stayed up last night, late, working on The Book. The little ones had been unusually restless, babbling and crying in their dreams. Teacher had gone from room to room, writing like mad, recording everything.

Even Hunter had talked in his sleep. What was it? Something about ghosts?

The Book was lying next to her, open to a page with a picture of a little girl on it. She was wearing a pink polka-dotty bathing suit and beaming, grinning happily up at the sun. *Protect her from the rays with Beach Babies!* the caption read. Across the bottom of the page was Teacher's own handwriting, in red ink: *BURNBURNBURNBURNBURN.*

Teacher slapped the book shut and rose up from the bed. The house was totally quiet—not even the sounds of Mommy making breakfast, such as it was these days. Applesauce slopped out in bowls, and Mommy's ritual, which she insisted upon, of placing neatly folded napkins at each place. Mommy had found the napkins in one of the drawers: pretty pale blue cloth, stitched in white with the initials *RFB.* Of course the napkins were old now and stained with beet juice and ripped up from the children's tug-of-war games.

Teacher's thoughts turned to the *B* people who must have owned the napkins and this house. And the *B* child—a girl?—who must have slept in this room, her room—the girl with the horse painting.

She shook her head, annoyed by the mental digression, and walked over to the window.

The storm had stopped. The sun was shining through wispy morning clouds. Teacher decided to go outside, before everyone was up, and collect some fresh rainwater from the reservoirs. She would mix up some Hi-C drink for breakfast and surprise the little ones.

She slapped on rubber flip-flops and headed downstairs. Outside, she found the water wagon in the carport, filled with empty milk jugs. The wagon was one of those red ones with a handle. Teacher remembered vaguely that she used to have one like it long ago, in the Before Time. *A little girl sitting on it with a rhinestone crown on her head.*

"Teacher?"

Teacher whirled around. Teddy Bear was standing there, wearing pajamas with tiny pink ballerinas on them. How had he snuck up on her? She hadn't heard a thing.

"When'd you get up?" she asked him.

"Just now." Teddy Bear rubbed his eyes and blinked sleepily at the wagon. "You collecting water? Can I come with you? Puh-leeease?"

Teacher was about to say no—she really preferred to do this particular activity alone—but then she sighed and said, as she always did with him, "Okay. Get your shoes."

Teddy Bear ran into the house. He came back a minute later with Teacher's red rain boots that were way too big for him. "Ready now."

The wheels of the rusty wagon squealed as Teacher yanked on the handle. She headed down the driveway and into the street, followed by Teddy Bear. His red rain boots made sloppy, squishy sounds as he walked.

The two of them proceeded down the street. Hunter and Action Figure had set up elaborate reservoirs and tanks at houses throughout the neighborhood. Teacher went to each one, used the plastic milk jugs to collect the water, and set them on the wagon. Teacher had long ago stopped noticing the emptiness of the houses, the wild overgrown lawns, the broken windows and roofs smashed during horrorcanes; the cars halted at odd angles on the streets, crashed into telephone poles and trees, reminders of the sudden terrible deaths.

She had even stopped noticing the stench of hot rotting garbage that rose from the swimming pools. In the First Year, the family had decided to start dumping all their trash in the pools to keep from attracting animals. It was so easy to do. After all, there were lots of pools in Lazarus, and, of course, there was nobody around to complain about it.

The whole time she worked, Teddy Bear didn't say a word, just followed. She could feel him near her, though, feel his hand reach up occasionally to tug on her dress. No, not even tug, but just touch it, almost as if to make sure she was still there.

Teacher knew Teddy Bear wanted to come along on these expeditions to make sure she wouldn't be eaten by an alligator. Which was annoying, since she didn't like having to think about alligators at all. She supposed she should be grateful to have an extra pair of eyes along. Still, it bothered her—his constant clinging protectiveness.

Nearby, there was a rustling in a bush.

Teddy Bear grabbed Teacher's leg. "Alligator," he whispered in a trembling voice.

"That is *not* an alligator," Teacher told him, exasperated.

"Alligator," Teddy Bear repeated, scrunching his small, thin body against her. She could feel his muscles going rigid.

Teacher sighed. "Look, that is not an alligator. I will prove it," she said. She reached down and peeled Teddy Bear off and began moving toward the bush.

Teddy Bear started screaming. "No! *No!*"

Just then, two little figures jumped out of the bush and scurried away. They disappeared behind a house.

Teacher stopped in her tracks, stunned. Behind her, Teddy Bear stopped screaming and said, "That wasn't no alligator."

The blue *RFB* napkins were stiff with food, but Mommy folded them and placed them on the table, one at each place. Baby, Doll, and Action Figure were sitting in their chairs, spooning beets into their mouths. Baby and Doll were naked, brown as berries. Action Figure was, too, except for a hand-crocheted afghan tied around his waist, like a skirt. His hair was thickly matted and snarled with leaves. He scratched his head with black-rimmed fingernails.

Doll propped her doll on the table. "Dolly hates beets!"

Baby banged her spoon on her bowl. "No more beets! No more beets!" she sang.

Action Figure began stabbing at his beets with the blade of his spoon. "Die, die, die!" he cried out, chopping the beets into tiny pieces. "Bad beets! Die! *Bam-bam!*"

Mommy sighed. "Please don't do that. It's all we have until lunchtime," she said to the children.

But they wouldn't stop. Mommy leaned against the counter, feeling dizzy all of a sudden. Sometimes, she had no idea what to do, what to say to them. They could be so wild, so out of control. Mommies were supposed to make their children behave. Mommies were also supposed to feed them, clothe them, soothe their nightmares. Make all their pain and sadness go away. Give them haircuts, brush their teeth, sing and sweet-talk.

She took a deep breath, then reached up to the shelf above the barren sink. She pulled down a cookbook: *Favorite Holiday Recipes.*

Mommy opened the cookbook. Many of the pages were missing, torn. She knew Teacher had gone through it for Information, clippings for The Book, just as she had with all the books and magazines and newspapers in the house.

After a minute, she found an intact page. "Listen to this!" she said to the children.

They stopped their noisy play for a second and listened, their faces upturned, their dried, cracked lips stained purply red with beet juice.

"Christmas pudding! Let's pretend we're eating Christmas pudding! 'Take one stick of butter and half a pound of chocolate.' Chocolate, isn't that wonderful?" Mommy cried out.

The children looked confused. "Chocklit, whassat?" Action Figure asked her.

"Hunter hunted some for us once, remember?" Mommy reminded them. "From Winn-Dixie. It's dark and sweet, sweet in your mouth like a lovely dream."

Doll made her dolly dance up and down on the counter. "Dolly wants chocklit."

"We're playing chocolate-pretend games," Mommy told her. "Let's pretend the beets are chocolate. Let's mix them all up in our bowls and make Christmas pudding!"

The children obeyed. They stirred their spoons in their bowls, sloshing the sliced canned beets around. Mommy felt a moment of happiness that she had calmed them down, but she also felt a pang in her heart, too. A terrible, achy pang that was always there, that would never go away.

The back door burst open. Teddy Bear rushed in, followed by Teacher.

The children stopped stirring and glanced up. "Where've you been?" Mommy asked Teddy Bear and Teacher.

"We saw kids," Teddy Bear announced. "Two of 'em!"

Mommy stared at Teacher. "Really?" she demanded.

"It was hard to tell," Teacher murmured, looking uncomfortable.

Mommy studied Teacher's face. She could always tell when Teacher was lying—like dealing with a little child, sometimes. "Did you or didn't see children?"

The back door opened again, and Hunter came in. He reached into his backpack and pulled a small white box out of it. "I hunted us some breakfast!" he said. "Ice cream cones, from the Quik-E-Mart!"

Action Figure ran over and scooped up the box from his brother's hands. He tore it open, took out a small brown cone, began gnawing at it. Baby and Doll did the same.

"We can pretend we're eating real ice cream!" Mommy said to the little ones in a loud, cheerful voice. Then she turned to Hunter and whispered, "Teacher and Teddy think they saw two kids."

"I didn't *say* that," Teacher insisted. She crossed her arms over her chest.

Teddy Bear stared up at her, his brown eyes enormous. Teacher noticed, then sighed. "Okay," she said. "Okay, maybe they could have been kids."

"I told you!" Hunter cried out to no one in particular. "I *told* you I saw kids!"

"But they might not have been, too!" Teacher said. "They could have been dogs or raccoons."

Mommy glanced at the little ones on the linoleum flour, devouring ice cream cones. "Would you like chocklit, manilla, or strawby?" Doll was saying to her dolly.

Then Mommy turned to Hunter and Teacher. "No one gets dogs and raccoons and kids mixed up," she said. "You saw kids. Two kids. And if they're out there, we have to get them!"

Chapter Three

After breakfast, Teacher sat at her desk, absently kicking the chair rungs as she turned the pages of The Book. Each page was a dense collage of yellowed, pasted-in clippings with an overlay of handwriting, so that headlines swam behind a thicket of other words, one after another catching her eye like something floating up through murky water.

KIDS UNDER TEN EAT FREE!
Buy Now, Pay Later

Rural Children Eat Few Vegetables, Study Shows

Pen poised, Teacher turned another thickly laminated page that made a popping sound as it turned: there were the 10 Commandments that she had collected and pasted in. On the next page, she began to write in the white space surrounding

Crop Losses Mean Higher Prices, Farm Group Warns.

There were two. I saw two. Teddy saw them first, but I had a better view of them. Their clothes were too big for them and very dirty.

Their hair was dirty and tangly, but not very
long. They've had haircuts? Maybe one is a
girl and one is a boy, but I can't really say
for sure because they disappeared too fast.

She ran out of blank space and skipped to the next page to write over a picture of a boy at a picnic table eating an ice cream cone. There was a First Mommy in the background of the picture, but she had been scribbled over so many times with the words *Come back* in different colors of ink that it was hard to make out anything of her features. Teacher continued writing.

I don't know where they coulda come from.
They haven't been here all the time or we
woulda seen them before. Mommy wants to
take care of them, but we can't. What if
there are even more? We can't hardly even
feed us. If Mommy decides to feed every
stray we'll all starve.

Except that they'd never seen any other strays. Not since those first few months, the First Year, when—well, when everything was very bad and so many lost children were dying. But Teacher and Mommy and Hunter and the others all found each other and became a family. Since then there hadn't been anyone else.

Restless, Teacher pushed her chair back and stood up. She wanted to talk to Mommy, but at the same time she didn't. What good would talking about it do? She knew Mommy was quite determined to get these strays somehow even though it was crazy, dumb, dangerous.

Hunter, well, Hunter was the one who got nearly all the food they ate, and his foraging expeditions were taking longer and longer all the time. It was rare these days that he found a real Bonus, like candy bars or popcorn, which they could pop on a wire screen over a charcoal fire.

At the window, Teacher looked down into the yard. The stray children she had seen must have been taken care of by somebody until not too long ago, but if they had gone wild, it could only be because that person was now gone. Gone meant dead.

Her breath moved the filmy curtain as she began to cry. How could they possibly feed anyone else?

Hunter found his brother in the driveway out in front of the house under the palm tree, where he was pouring swampy swimming pool water from a cup into an anthill. The red ants were crawling frantically in all directions, some caught up in the streams that ran through the sand, some carrying little white beads. Action Figure, dressed only in ragged denim shorts and oversized men's boots, squatted on his haunches, staring at the ants. Hunter put his hands on his knees and leaned over to see; he had to squint to see what it was, and then the sight of the scurrying ants made him suddenly feel sick.

"Come on," he said, standing up abruptly. His head swam with dizziness, and he had to grab Action Figure's shoulder for a moment until he caught his balance. "I got a surprise for you."

His little brother turned to peer up at him through matted, sun-whitened bangs. His face and chest and arms were tanned as dark as a coconut from playing outside all the time: Teacher could almost never rope him into a class. When she did, he usually jumped out a window and ran off.

"Whatcha got?" the boy asked.

"Surprise," Hunter repeated, leading the way through the carport and through the gate to the backyard while Action Figure followed, clumping behind him in his big boots. The green scum on the surface of the swimming pool undulated in the afternoon breeze. Near the shallow end was an open patch of water with jagged edges, as though someone had dropped a bulky object into the pool. Tucked into a corner of the fence was a storage shed that sagged with rot. Hunter jerked open the door, scraping it over the sandy grass.

"Surprise in 'ere?" Action Figure asked, his green eyes widening.

Hunter grinned, and reached into the musty dimness of the shed. "I found these in a store of sports stuff."

Triumphant, he pulled out his treasure and held it aloft for his brother to see: a bow and arrow set. Action Figure took one look and let out a crow of delight, leaping up and grabbing it out of Hunter's hands and bearing it off with glee. He whooped and screeched, hopping from foot to foot and waving his new weapons over his head. Hunter watched him for a moment, grinning.

"Let's try it out, 'kay?" he suggested.

Action Figure ran back, and together they ripped off the plastic and tore the bow and arrows out of the box. "Have to learn to use it carefully," Hunter warned, trying not to let his own excitement show.

"Ya-ya-ya," Action Figure agreed.

The smile on the young boy's face was so full of joy that Hunter felt pride surge through him and make him strong. He had done this. He had gone hunting and caught happiness for his brother. It was good.

"Now I'm a hunter, too," Action Figure said as he picked up the bow and twanged the string.

"Not right away," Hunter hastened to say.

"You never lemme go," Action Figure complained.

Hunter picked up the arrows and didn't answer. He never let anyone go with him; too many bones. He was used to it, but he didn't want his brother or any of the others to see the skulls and long leg bones and other things—fingers and other bits, teeth. He had removed them all from the places he went the most, and from the neighborhood they lived in. But a turn down a discovered alleyway or the back door of a newly explored house would always turn up skeletons. Always. It wouldn't be good for the older kids to be reminded of the days of Fire-us. He wasn't even sure the little ones remembered anything at all, so he especially didn't want them to see the bones and start to ask questions.

"You don' lemme," Action Figure repeated, and a sly look crossed his face. "But I folla sometime."

Hunter had been testing the sharpness of the arrowheads, rubbing his calloused thumb over the tips, but he whipped around to look at his brother when he heard that. "You follow me yesterday? Before the storm started?"

Something in his voice made Action Figure back away. "No."

"You didn't follow me into the supermarket?"

Action Figure thrust out his chin, brave again. "I say

no!" He pouted. "Gimme arras."

Reluctant, Hunter handed the arrows to his brother, and stood beside him to help him nock the arrow to the string. He noticed with surprise that Action Figure came up to his shoulder, now. Getting bigger. "Here, do like this."

"Wait!" Action Figure dropped the bow and dug into the pocket of his shorts. "Foundis. Good for superhero eyes."

With some effort, he untangled a pair of eyeglasses from the mess of junk in his pocket. They had thick lenses, and the brown plastic rims were cracked and almost falling into two pieces. Action Figure opened them up and put them on, and turned his face up to peer at the sky.

Hunter let out a shout of laughter. "You look like a bug!"

"Do not." Action Figure bent to pat around on the ground, aiming for and missing a grab at the bow.

"It ain't superhero eyes if you can't see what you're looking at," Hunter said. "Here, let me try 'em."

He plucked them off his brother's face and put them on his own.

His heart gave a giant knock in his chest as he looked up and around himself. He could see with a clarity he'd never known: sharp edge of palm frond, tiny leaf of alga, grain of sand, blade of grass, thread of Spanish moss. Sweat broke out on his forehead.

"Givum back," Action Figure said. "Thass mine."

Hunter didn't answer, but stood gazing at everything, stunned, almost frightened by the crispness of his eyesight. It was like a magical thing. He had never known this.

Then, in an instant, Action Figure snatched the glasses away. By reflex Hunter made a wild grab for them. The two boys struggled over them, and then there was a sharp snap and they were broken in two.

Action Figure glared at the lens and earpiece in his hand, and with a scowl of disgust tossed them into the scummy pool. They landed with a muffled plop and then sank below the green surface, leaving a quivery hole.

Hunter gaped at his brother, a cry rising up through him. Already, Action Figure had forgotten about his superhero glasses and was snapping the bowstring, his head bent over the bow and his white-streaked hair falling like a curtain in front of his face. Swallowing his disappointment, Hunter closed his fingers around the remaining lens. It was suddenly the most valuable thing in his world, and his little brother had been the one to hunt it down.

Mommy opened a jar of applesauce, grunting with the effort of breaking the vacuum. She let it flow and flop into the paper bowls lined up on the counter while Teacher stood at the door, watching Hunter and Action Figure. To Mommy, Teacher's back communicated loud and clear a message of stubborn anger. She chose to ignore it. "How long before we can't stand the taste of applesauce, do you think," she asked, keeping her tone light.

Teacher jerked one shoulder: more obvious resentment. "We'll run out of it before we get sick of it," she muttered.

"No we won't."

"We will."

Mommy slammed the jar down on the counter. She could be stubborn, too. "We won't run out. Hunter will find more. He can find anything."

Teacher turned around, looking as though she was prepared to keep fighting forever, but the sound of running feet stopped her. She looked away as the little ones bumbled into the kitchen. Teddy Bear, Baby, and Doll had all dressed themselves in ladies' bathing suits, which bagged around their skinny bodies. They had all fashioned belts out of curly phone cords, and Doll's stained and one-eyed doll was riding papooselike in the gaping back of Doll's costume. In spite of their ages they acted like much younger children, like kindergartners. Mommy sometimes wondered if she was right about that—they were supposed to be more Grown-up by now, weren't they? And if they were, did that mean she wasn't a good enough mother for them? This was what worried her—that she was doing something wrong. She tried her best, but maybe there was something really important she didn't know about.

"Dinner," Mommy announced. "Someone call Hunter and Action."

"I'll do it." Teacher pushed open the screen door with her folded arms and stepped out into the backyard.

The little girls and Teddy Bear hitched themselves up onto their chairs. Baby's face was striped red and blue with makeup that Hunter had scavenged for her. Doll reached over her shoulder as she sat down, grabbed her dolly by the hair, and whipped it out. She tossed it onto the table and began to sing to it.

"Baby see the ear of Jean. Hey, I'm Jake, Hey!

Elemenopy! Cue or us, there you be. Double you asked why and zeed."

"That's what you learn in elemenopy school, right?" Baby asked Mommy.

"That's right." Mommy set bowls of applesauce in front of the children and opened a box of white and gold plastic spoons with *Our Wedding* written on the handles. She heard Teacher talking with the boys outside as Baby picked among the pile of identical spoons until she found one that suited her.

Baby looked up at Mommy again. "And elemenopy school is where there are lots of other children too, right?"

"That's right."

The door opened, and Teacher came back inside. Mommy looked at Teacher and felt an impulse to provoke the fight out into the open. She smiled at Teddy Bear as Action Figure clomped into the kitchen in his oversized boots, dragging his bow and arrows. "And did you tell the girls about the wild children you saw today, Teddy? No weapons in the house, Action," she added.

Action Figure opened the door and tossed his gear out into the carport. "Wild childrum? I'll catchum."

"No, you won't," Teacher snapped.

"Will too. Make a trap." Action Figure crouched in his chair and dragged a full bowl toward himself and shoveled applesauce into his mouth while he kept his chin on the table.

Doll's eyes widened. "Action isn't doing Manners," she said.

Teacher reached across the table and gave Action Figure a light smack on his rear end, reminding him to sit nicely in his chair. She shot an angry look at Mommy. "I thought we weren't going to discuss this until later."

"I don't know what there is to discuss. It's obvious we have to get them."

Mommy felt as though she might begin screaming or throwing things. It was a scary, out-of-control spirit that stole into her sometimes and made her want to smash a window. She took a few deep breaths. The door opened again, and Hunter came in and took a seat at the table. With another deep and shuddery breath Mommy swiped one hand across her nose, and poured clean water into the applesauce jar. She tightened the lid, and shook the jar.

"Can you really catch them wild kids?" Teddy Bear asked Action Figure and Hunter. "I seen 'em. They can run away real good."

"We could set out some bait," Hunter offered.

He didn't take any applesauce, Mommy noticed, but watched the little children spoon it in. She winced. She hadn't realized how thin he had become, hadn't realized she wasn't the only one skipping meals. Her own stomach growled as she poured the appley water into paper cups. "Juice," she said.

"We can't afford it!" Teacher burst out. Table chatter stopped and everyone stared at her. "We don't have enough for ourselves! If we leave food outside it's like we're just throwing it away."

Again, Mommy felt the screaming spirit race in her heart with spears and fire. She gripped the counter's edge and tried to breathe deep enough to drive it away. She saw Hunter glance at her, and she turned away from them all, fighting for calm.

"I'll find more food," Hunter said in a low voice. "I'll

just go farther away. I can make overnight trips, find some other towns. There's gotta be something."

At the table, the little ones were happy again, licking their bowls and tapping out a rhythm on their cups with their plastic spoons. Doll began singing her Baby-Sees to her dolly once more. Teacher had her head in her hands, rocking it from side to side. Mommy looked out the window over the sink, into the rank jungle of the backyard with its tangle of rotting flowers and algae-thickened pool. She wondered if they were all going to die.

And then, without warning, the knocker on the front door banged three times.

Chapter Four

Everyone froze.

Mommy stood very still, her knuckles whitening where they gripped the counter. She thought, *It's the hunger—I'm hearing things.* But then the knocker banged again, *bangbangbangbangbangbang,* more loud and insistent this time.

It was a sound they hadn't heard in five years. In more than five years, not since the Before Time when there were Visitors and Relatives and Children-coming-over-to-play. But this wasn't even a *bangbang* like that, but an angry *bangbang.* Like someone bad, like someone bad coming to get them all.

Behind her, Baby began to cry. Mommy felt the cry deep in her belly and rushed over to comfort her. Doll started crying, too, and Mommy wrapped her arms around the both of them, around their bony brown bodies in the sagging ladies' bathing suits. Dolly fell to the floor, and her one good eye blinked once and then stared blankly up at the ceiling.

Teacher sat at the table, her gaze fixed on the door. Teddy Bear tried to climb into her lap, but there was no space between her body and the hard edge of the table. "Alligator," he whispered, clutching and clawing at Teacher's legs. *"Alligator!"* But Teacher was gazing at the door, as if in a trance, and didn't seem to hear him.

"It must be the strays," Hunter said in a loud voice.

Mommy could see that he was trying to be brave.

"Wild childrum!" Action Figure cried out. He glanced around, and grabbed a paring knife off the counter. It was stained purply red from the morning's beets, which Mommy had sliced extrathin in an effort to stretch the last jar. "Round 'em up and catchum," he said, tucking the knife into the waistband of his denim shorts. "Put 'em inna cage!"

"Action Figure!" Mommy scolded. "Put the knife back. Now!"

Action Figure obeyed, sulking. Hunter turned to Mommy. "I'll get the door, then?" he said.

"No." Mommy lifted the hem of her powder blue T-shirt—MY PARENTS WENT TO TAMPA, AND ALL THEY BROUGHT BACK WAS THIS LOUSY T-SHIRT!—and wiped the dirty, tearstained faces of Baby and Doll, their runny noses. The door banged again and everyone jumped as though in pain. Mommy sucked in a deep breath and rose to her feet. "I'll get it."

Hunter was about to protest, but Mommy raised her hand to shush him. "It's okay. You stay with the children," she added, glancing at Teacher, who seemed to be in her own world and not capable of dealing with the little ones at all.

Then Teacher began to speak: "Where's The Book? Gotta read it, gotta see what it says, then we'll know what to do. That's right. The Book'll tell us what to do. Ten Commandments. Number One: Accept No Substitutes. Number Two: Just Say No to Drugs."

Baby and Doll began crying again. Teddy Bear began crying, too. At the door, the *bangbangbang* started up again. *Bang. Bang. BANG!* And then, silence.

"Everyone, please . . . Teacher, stop it, you're upsetting the children! Hunter, isn't there a Bonus you can scare up, maybe in the back of the cupboards?" Mommy remembered that there were a few pieces of dried-up rock-hard bubble gum hidden away somewhere. "Everyone just stay here, please, while I see who's at the door. Hunter, don't let anyone leave the kitchen. I'm going to . . . take care of this."

And with that, she took another deep breath and started walking toward the front door.

Mommy knew it wasn't going to be the strays on the other side. Little ones wouldn't knock on a door like that, with such force. For that matter, they wouldn't be able to reach the knocker, so high up.

So who was it? Fear coursed through her veins like ice water, and her heart hammered in her chest, thrummed in her ears. Still, she managed to compose a smile on her face, go through the motion of wiping her hands on the hem of her T-shirt. As though she'd been caught in the middle of doing the dishes.

Someone I know used to do that, she thought as she reached the front hall, put her hand on the doorknob, opened the door.

She stifled a scream.

It was a Grown-up.

Mommy did a double take. It was *not* a Grown-up. It was a very tall boy, taller than Hunter, standing in the evening shadows. He had long, straggly dark brown hair that went past his shoulders. He was wearing a grimy white button-down shirt with the sleeves ripped off and khakis with one leg entirely gone. A maroon silk tie with thin blue stripes was wrapped around his head, like a bandanna.

The boy was holding a long, badly frayed rope. Tethered to the other end of it was—no, not a dead body, but a naked, full-sized mannequin. Like the ones from Myer's department store, in the Before Time. This one, the boy's, had unblinking amber eyes and fakey-smooth beige skin and no hair at all. A man mannequin with no thingy between his legs.

In the boy's other hand was a beaten-up old wooden picture frame. He held it up now to his thin, handsome face and smiled—or rather, parted his pale, cracked lips, as if on cue—and revealed perfectly straight but slightly chipped teeth.

"Good evening! And now the news," the boy said in a pleasant voice.

Mommy stepped backward with a gasp, and grasped for the edge of a chair, a table, anything to hold on to.

"Today in Washington, the Pentagon announced that it would be testing a new high-speed interceptor capable of destroying multiple warheads in space," the boy recited through the picture frame. His dark, dark eyes were fixed on some point past Mommy's shoulder, and his voice was crisp, smart, professional—a Grown-up's voice. "Hundreds of antinuclear demonstrators protested the controversial program, estimated to cost taxpayers at least a hundred billion dollars over the next two years.

"And at the Centers for Disease Control in Atlanta, scientists announced a new vaccine to combat the dreaded vir—the dreaded . . . *damn* it, wrong cue card! That's right, *that* one! Yes! Excuse me, folks. . . . Wait, we're breaking up the transmission a little bit, Jason? Can you hear me? Yes, okay, we're still here.

"And now on the local front. In downtown Fort Myers,

a family of alligators kicked off their three-day weekend by feasting on a couple of recently deceased grandmothers. Yum-yum! *Bon appétit*, guys!"

Mommy clapped a hand to her mouth. She felt herself go all cold inside, all cold and clammy and nauseous. This boy was a lunatic, an angry and dangerous lunatic, and she had opened the door to him. Clearly, he was going to kill them all. Kill her little babies, kill Hunter, kill Teacher, kill her.

Mommy heard a soft shuffling noise behind her, and turned around. They had all crept into the front hall and were staring at the crazy lunatic murderous boy in the doorway. Teddy Bear was clinging to Teacher's sundress and sucking hard on his thumb, drool cascading everywhere. Action Figure had the paring knife again, was clutching the purply-red blade between his teeth. Baby and Doll were holding each of Hunter's hands, chomping on bubble gum, grinning at the boy as though he were some sort of very interesting new toy.

"More news on the local front!" the boy went on. "Two strange children were spotted today in the vicinity. A little boy and a little girl."

"What?" Mommy whipped around. "What did you say?"

But the boy didn't appear to hear her. "Coming up after this commercial break, the weather!" He turned his head to the side, directed his smile at the nearly dead oleander bushes at the side of the front stoop. "Marge, I have a feeling it's going to be another bea-uuutiful weekend!"

Then the boy lowered the picture frame from his face and fixed his nearly-black eyes on Mommy. The eyes, she thought, were the most startling thing about him. So full of rage.

"Got anything to eat?" he asked all of a sudden, not in the newscaster's voice, but in a regular kid's voice.

Before Mommy could speak, she felt the children rushing, swarming around her legs. "Who are you?" Baby demanded. "Are you Santy Claus?"

"Did you bring me a new dolly?" Doll added, pointing to the mannequin.

Action Figure extracted the beet-stained paring knife from between his teeth, waved it at the boy. "I'm a superhero, bam-bam! Wanna play combat games?"

"Action!" Mommy exclaimed.

"Identify yourself," Hunter told the boy. Stern, manly, hands on hips. "What are you doing here at our house? Who are you?"

"The Book, gotta get The Book," Teacher began chanting, rocking back and forth on her heels.

Teddy Bear, still clutching Teacher's dress, extracted his thumb from his mouth and burst into tears again.

While Teddy Bear cried, Baby, Doll, and Hunter continued barraging the boy with questions. Mommy put her hands over her ears and closed her eyes. It was too much, too much. It was all spinning out of control.

And then in the next second she opened her eyes, reached out, and corralled Baby, Doll, Action Figure, the sobbing Teddy Bear. "Upstairs, all of you. To bed!"

"No, Mommy!" Baby wailed. "Not yet!"

"Puh-lease, just a little while longer?" Doll begged.

"Absolutely not. Up to bed." Mommy ushered the four children toward the stairs. "Hunter, you give . . . you give that guy some dinner," she called over her shoulder.

"Teacher, please help Hunter. I'm putting the children to bed. And when I get back downstairs, we're going to have a good long talk," she said to the strange boy.

Mommy pushed the four little ones upstairs—Baby and Doll and Action wriggling and uncooperative, Teddy Bear still shuddering with sobs—and breathed, just breathed, trying in vain to compose herself for whatever lay ahead.

Hunter crossed his arms over his chest and circled the subject, who sat at the kitchen table. The mannequin leaned like a plank across a chair next to him. The subject was eating the stale ice cream cones, the ones Hunter had hunted at the Quik-E-Mart. Two at a time, almost inhaling them. Crumbs everywhere. Mommy wouldn't be happy.

Teacher had stopped her rantings about The Book and was standing at the sink. All quiet, watching while Hunter conducted the debriefing. She had a scrap of paper towel in her hand and a pen, and was taking notes.

Hunter demanded, "Name, rank, Cereo number."

The boy didn't answer, just continued inhaling the ice cream cones.

"I said, name, rank, Cereo number!" Louder this time. Clearly the subject had problems respecting authority.

The subject glanced up, held the beat-up picture frame up to his face and smiled. "News at eleven!" he said in that weird, Grown-up voice of his. Then, lowering the frame, he added, "Got any soda?" That, in the kid's voice.

Teacher stopped writing and spoke up. "We don't have soda. All we've got is water and Hi-C mix."

"Hi-C?" The subject said the word wondrously, breathed it as if it were the name of some valuable treasure.

"Can I *have* some?"

Teacher glanced at Hunter, shrugged, then walked over to the cupboard to get the can of mix.

While Teacher prepared the Hi-C, Hunter studied the subject. He wished he could take his magic lens out, *really* study him. But he was too nervous to do it, with Teacher there and everything.

In any case, Hunter was not happy about the subject's presence. The subject was an intruder in their household, possibly unstable. *Definitely* unstable. Fortunately, this would just be a temporary situation. The subject was going to have to be sent packing after the debriefing. There wasn't room in their household for *two* men. It had always been just him, Mommy, and Teacher taking care of the little ones, and it was going to stay that way.

He heard Mommy's footsteps then, on the stairs. A moment later she appeared in the kitchen, pale and squeezing her fingers into fists. "The children are in bed," she announced. "What's going on?" she asked Hunter, although her eyes were fixed on the subject.

Just then, the subject raised the picture frame to his face again. "And now, we'll be taking questions from the studio audience!" he said with a smile.

Teacher set a paper cup full of thin, orangey Hi-C in front of him. He picked it up, drank it down in one thirsty gulp. Then Teacher got her pen and paper towel and prepared to take notes again. "*I* have a question. What's with the mannequin?"

The subject turned to the naked mannequin. "This is Bad Guy," he said by way of formal introduction. Then, without warning, he let out a horrible cry and slammed Bad Guy to the floor.

Hunter, Teacher, and Mommy stared at him and then at each other.

"Why'd you do that?" Mommy whispered, breaking the silence.

"This is Bad Guy," the subject repeated, lowering the picture frame. He had bitten his lip, and there was a drop of blood trickling down his chin. "You know, Bad Guy. The guy who made the virus."

Hunter wasn't expecting this. His glance darted to Mommy and away. "W-we don't talk about that," he said. "About the Fire-us."

But the subject ignored him. He held the picture frame up to his face. Smiling through clenched teeth, he said, "All around the world, people died in great agony as the mysterious virus—excuse me, Fire-us—brought on fevers of 107, 108, 109 Fahrenheit. Inner organs boiling, melting. Within a week, most of the adult population of the world had been wiped out. Bodies everywhere, corpses. The stinking horrible smell of them! Children running around the streets, suddenly orphans. Most of them died, too, from famine and disease and . . . well, *just bein' orphans*. You know how it is, folks! That orphan thing, it's a real bummer. That Destruction of the World thing, too, and that Make-Way-for-the-Second-Whatchamacallit thing! And . . . it's . . . all . . . be . . . cause . . . of . . . *Him!*"

The subject stopped talking for a second and kicked the mannequin in the stomach. The mannequin skidded across the linoleum floor, banged into the Chef-Magik electric stove and stopped there.

A long, terrible silence.

Hunter felt ill all of a sudden. They never talked about Fire-us, *never*. He could see that Mommy and Teacher looked ill, too. The subject was going to have to go, now, even before the debriefing was over. He was a disruptive force, a Bad Influence.

But then Mommy sighed and dabbed at her eyes and said, "Let's all just go to sleep, okay, and we'll talk about this in the morning."

What? Hunter turned to Mommy, stunned. "You mean . . . he's going to sleep here?"

"It's late," Mommy said. "He can sleep in the living room on the couch. What's your name, anyway?" she asked the subject.

"Anchorman," he replied.

There was no more discussion. Mommy and Teacher proceeded upstairs. Anchorman wiped the ice cream cone crumbs from his face, the blood from his lip. He picked Bad Guy off the floor and headed into the living room, dragging the mannequin behind him.

Hunter followed Mommy and Teacher. Halfway up the stairs, he paused. Above him, he could hear Baby call out sleepily from the bed she and Doll shared with Mommy: "Mommy? Is that boy really Santy Claus?"

"His name's Anchorman," Hunter heard Mommy say. "Hush now, go to sleep."

No one looking. Hunter pulled the magic lens out of his pocket, turned, snuck a last peek at the subject.

In the living room, Anchorman was tying Bad Guy to a chair with the rope, swiveling the rigid legs so they stuck straight out. When he was finished, he settled into another chair, upright, as if intending to keep watch over the mannequin for the rest of the night.

Chapter Five

Somewhere out in the night an owl hooted, and there was a tiny animal scream as something died. Teacher rolled onto her side, propping her head on her outstretched arm, and stared at the pale rectangle of the window where the stars faintly showed. Another night when she knew she would have no sleep. A mosquito whined over her head. Definitely, she would not sleep.

With a sigh, she pushed back the sheet and padded across the room, feeling on the desk for her flashlight. Her fingers closed around the handle, and she switched it on and then tucked it under her chin so that she could shine its beam onto The Book. A sign. There must be one somewhere in those heavy pages. This Anchorman frightened her.

The headings from the book of Yellow Pages filled one whole section, each one cut out as a strip, like those sayings they used to find sometimes inside folded China cookies. She scanned the headings, letting her mind skim over their meanings as the light passed over the words. This was how the signs came to her.

Refrigerators—Research. Home—Hospital. Carpet— Cat. Swimming—Tailors. Toys—Travel.

She paused over *Toys—Travel,* and noted that it would be a good lesson plan for School. Then the memory of Anchorman's wild voice came in her ear, and she continued searching.

Water—Weights. Teacher frowned. Did this have a meaning? Clean water was important, and it was heavy. Then her eyes were caught by *Mountain—Movers.*

He could move mountains, the First Mommy said, laughing and shaking her head about something or someone. He won't let anything get in his way.

That memory flickered into Teacher's mind and was gone before she could grasp it and hang on. She tried to bring it back, to savor that voice, that Grown-up voice. But it was no use. She shook her head and tried to concentrate on the meaning. It was the sign she was looking for. Anchorman could move mountains.

But she didn't know what that meant for their family, or even if it mattered.

This was the trouble with The Book. It only gave partial answers. Teacher often felt frightened of The Book, or even angry with it. She wasn't sure she was the right person to try to understand its meanings. It was so confusing so much of the time. If there was only a Grown-up . . .

But there wasn't.

Teacher shut The Book and switched off her flashlight. That was all she would learn about Anchorman tonight. But she also knew she was not going to be able to sleep.

From down the hall came a muffled whimper. Teacher cocked her head to listen. It was Mommy, talking in her sleep. Teacher waited to hear if it would be a long talking dream, one that she needed to write down. She heard Mommy say the word *Fire-us* very clearly and then subside into mutters and soft cries. It wouldn't be loud enough to wake Doll and Baby. Teacher squared her thin shoulders as she stood in the doorway waiting for more news from Mommy. But the next room was silent again. She fanned her sweaty face with her hand and waved aside a mosquito.

Now she paced, glancing out the window at the darkness of Lazarus. Where were those little wild children right now? Where were they huddling this dark night? Were they frightened? Did they ever say the word *Fire-us* in their dreams? Did they understand anything that had happened?

The thought of those small ones out in the dark made Teacher's heart race and her breath come short, as though she had been running, running. A sob rose up in her throat.

Then she rushed out of her room and felt her way down the dark hall, down the stairs, running her hand along the wall. In the kitchen she felt for the flashlight they always kept beside the sink, and clicked it on. The blade of light fell on the box of ice cream cones.

"I'm so stupid," Teacher said under her breath, even as she pulled two ice cream cones out of the box and crumbled them into a paper bowl. "I'm so stupid."

Dish in hand, she tiptoed to the front door, and opened it onto the darkness of the driveway, the palm trees, the deeper shadows of the overgrown oleanders that crowded in along the sides and the black massive hulk of the banyan. Night noises were all around her: frogs, insects, wind rubbing the stiff palms together. Teacher stood there, the cement step cool against her bare feet. A night lizard scuttled past her ankle and dove into the bushes.

Then Teacher bent down and placed the bowl of ice

cream cone pieces on the step, backed inside, and shut the door.

When Mommy opened her eyes in the morning, she had that delicious feeling of contentment that came from sleeping well. She rubbed her face against the pillow, pointed her toes, and took a deep breath.

And the next moment, the feeling had vanished, just as it always did.

Beside her, snuggled deep under the covers, were Baby and Doll. Mommy moved the sheets aside to look at them. Baby's eyes were squeezed shut tight as though she were concentrating on something in her sleep. Doll hugged her dolly against herself as she lay in a tightly curled ball. Both girls' sun-streaked hair lay in tangled wisps around their heads. Mommy felt her heart clench like a fist as she looked at them. She loved them so much. Looking at them was sometimes the most terrifying part of her day.

Doll let out a little grunt and flung herself over onto her other side, and then suddenly opened her eyes.

"Good morning," Mommy said, smiling.

Baby squeezed her eyes even more tightly as Doll wriggled up into a sitting position. Doll put her arms around Mommy's neck and hugged her.

"Is that Angerman still here?" Doll asked, her voice creaky with sleep.

Mommy laughed. "*Anchor*man. I think so."

"Can we go see him?" the little girl continued with a yawn.

Baby opened her eyes and pushed her hair away from her face. "What are you talking about?"

"Angerman slept here," Doll told Baby in her know-it-all way.

"Anchorman," Mommy repeated. "He said his name is Anchorman."

Doll pursed her lips and gave Mommy a pitying look. "Mommy, that doesn't mean anything. He's angry. So his name gotta be Angerman."

"But he's not an—" Mommy frowned. He *did* seem angry. Furiously angry. Maybe Doll was right.

Doll took Baby by the hand. "We're going to go look at him."

"He's not a freak show," Mommy said, although now that she thought about it, he sort of was. He was angry and he was freaky. She wasn't so sure she wanted him to still be there. "Get dressed and you can go downstairs."

The suggestion to get dressed was one that Mommy loved to make, because she never knew how the girls would meet the challenge. Over the years, Hunter had scavenged for real children's clothes, but all of the younger kids preferred making up their own wardrobes from things found around town. They used to heap all the clothes in a pile in a spare room, but one time Mommy had found mice nesting in the jumble. So now she tried to get the children to keep their clothes in drawers and on hangers, although they didn't very often. Mommy also made sure to throw clothes out when they got to be too dirty. They had no way to launder them— or at least they could, but it was a big waste of water when there were all the clothes in the world to replace them with, after all. So they all dressed themselves from a changing assortment of odds and ends scrounged from houses and shops all over Lazarus.

Now Doll was putting on a football jersey labeled MIAMI DOLPHINS and a lacy half-slip, and Baby was dressing herself in a polka-dotted hospital gown that wrapped around and tied with a straggly bit of twill tape. Neither of them bothered with shoes: their feet were as tough and calloused as leather anyway. They chattered together as they dressed, each pretending they knew things about Angerman that the other one didn't. Mommy put on a blue-and-yellow striped T-shirt and a pair of denim overalls, and followed the girls down the stairs.

He was there. He was slumped in an easy chair in the living room, his head tipped back and his mouth hanging open in sleep. The empty picture frame dangled from his drooping hand. Across from him, folded onto a chair pulled from the dining room, was that mannequin, its legs and arms jutting stiffly toward the front. It was bound like a prisoner. Like someone who could do harm to another person. Only this wasn't a person. It was just a plastic body with a plastic man's head.

As Mommy stood contemplating this strange sight, Baby and Doll climbed onto Angerman's lap. He woke up with a jerk.

"Wha—?" He looked wildly around, as though astonished to find himself in a house with two little girls sitting on his lap.

"What's this for?" Baby asked, reaching for the picture frame.

Angerman held it in front of her face to frame it, and he smiled at her. "This is so I always can see the best view," he said flirtatiously. He moved it to frame

Doll's face. "Two best views."

Both girls giggled, and Baby moved a bit as though to start edging Doll off Angerman's lap. "Where'dja come from?" she asked.

"I come from south of the sunshine," he teased. "Come here, tell me your names."

Mommy crossed her arms in front of her chest, watching him charm her girls. They seemed completely at home with him, despite his strangeness. She felt a twinge of something that might have been jealousy.

"They think your name is Angerman," she said, raising her voice over the excited chatter of Baby and Doll.

He was pushing himself up out of the chair, with a girl tucked under each arm. They shrieked with delight as he tried to hoist them up, gorilla-style. "How old are you two?" he asked, ignoring Mommy.

"We know!" Baby said breathlessly. "We have a Grow Up."

"What's that? Show me," he said as he set them down.

Doll and Baby began tugging on his hands, leading him up the stairs. Mommy listened to their noisy progress up the steps to the door of Teacher's bedroom. Inside the frame of Teacher's door was a series of lines and dates in colored ink. "April 2, 1993: 2 years old." "April 2, 1994: 3 years old," and so forth all the way up to the year 2002. There were no marks after that. Baby and Doll were both about at the eight-years-old mark. Mommy stood at the bottom of the stairs, lost in her thoughts. Small footsteps thudded as the girls ran into the boys' room.

"Are they your sisters?" Angerman asked, coming down the stairs again.

She pushed herself back from the banister to get out of his way. She didn't want him to brush past and accidentally touch her. "I found them."

He said nothing, and the silence stretched so long that Mommy had to look up at him. He wore an expression of terrible sadness.

"In the First Year," she added.

Angerman nodded, and his gaze strayed across the living room to the mannequin tied to its chair. He looked as though he might say something, but then he changed his mind, set his jaw, and walked away.

One of their battery-powered clocks said 8:30. One said 9:10. Another said 9:35. Whatever time it actually was never really mattered anyway. Teacher set pencils and lined paper out on the dining room table, and gave a blast on the dented trumpet that served as their school bell.

"Time for class!" she shouted.

There was a pounding of footsteps and some thumps. From the corner of her eye, Teacher saw Action Figure disappear through a window and scramble away. Bushes and branches outside the window shook and rustled as he pushed through them to escape. A moment later, Teddy Bear was there in the dining room. He was like that: silent as a mouse. One moment the room would be empty, and then a moment later you'd see that Teddy Bear was there. He pulled out a chair and climbed onto it, giving Teacher a tentative smile.

"Good morning, Teacher," he whispered, as though

he hadn't already seen her at breakfast time.

"Hi, Teddy. How are you today?"

Baby and Doll came in, carrying a bucket of scummy swimming pool water between them. Water slopped over the edges of the pail as they made their way to the table, leaving splatters on the floor. Teacher didn't bother to ask what it was for. In the living room, Hunter and Angerman and Mommy were deep in conversation, something about the wild children. While the kids settled themselves at the table, Hunter led Angerman out to the hallway; it sounded as though they were going into town. Teacher took The Book out of the pillowcase she always carried it in whenever she removed it from her bedroom and placed it reverently on the table. The children regarded it in respectful silence, their eyes wide. They would never touch it unless she gave them the signal that it was okay.

"Today's lesson is going—" Teacher began.

"Hey!" Hunter called from the front door. "Who left this dish of ice cream cones out here? It's all covered in ants."

Heat spread up Teacher's throat, and she jutted her chin out, keeping her eyes on the kids. "Today's lesson is Toys—Travel," she announced. "Here's what I want to show you."

Baby, Doll, and Teddy Bear all hitched themselves across the tabletop to look at page 29 of The Book. Teacher studied their faces as they looked at the picture: it was a magazine page with torn edges, and showed a Christmas tree sparkling with lights and ornaments, and a little boy in footed pajamas, sitting cross-legged in the center of an elaborate train set.

Teddy Bear was frowning, as though trying very hard to understand something without having to ask any questions. Baby stuck out one finger and pointed to the angel on the top of the tree, her finger hovering just over the page. Doll had been holding her dolly to look at the picture, but for some reason now turned the dolly's face away and pressed it against her skinny chest.

"This a train, see? In the Before Time people used to ride in trains," Teacher began. "Children with their First Mommies and Daddies would go to the train station and get on the train, and it would take them on the railroad tracks to a place they wanted to travel."

Baby's finger curled into her palm, and she pulled her hand away from the treetop angel. "How did they do that?"

"They got inside and sat in the seats," Teacher said.

"But it's little. How did the people get inside it?"

Teacher bit her lip. "Oh. Well, they were very, very big. See, this is a toy train. Remember? Our lesson is Toys—Travel. This is a toy pretend train, and this little boy is playing make-believe that he's traveling."

"To Baltimore," Teddy Bear said in a tiny voice.

Goose bumps rose on Teacher's arms. She swallowed once. Twice. "What did you say?"

He looked up, his brown eyes wide and moist. "He's pretending he's taking the train to Baltimore," he said in an even tinier voice.

Teacher felt a sensation like a wave rushing toward her.

There was an echoing train station, where the columns soared up into the ceiling like trees. Wooden benches like church pews were in rows at one side of the great waiting room, and announcements came over the loudspeakers, muffled and distorted like someone talking underwater.

There were five of them. The Mommy, the Daddy, the big sister, the little brother, and the baby sister, who toddled back and forth from the bench they sat on to the bench across from them, slapping her hands on the seats. The Mommy was reading papers from a briefcase, and the Daddy talked into a tiny folding telephone that he kept snapping shut and opening again, punching in numbers. The big sister looked up at the signboard, which clicked and flashed the names of cities, times, and track numbers.

A man in a white dress walked through the crowded train station, shouting in an angry voice with spit flying out of his mouth, and people moved away from him as though he smelled bad. The little brother walked away from the family, watching the man in the white dress who shouted, and the big sister ran after him and caught him by the hand, and he looked up at her with wide, questioning eyes.

"Teacher?" Baby tugged at Teacher's sleeve.

"What?" Shuddering, Teacher rubbed her hands together and dropped her head as though she was studying The Book.

From under her lashes, she looked at Teddy Bear, and then looked away again.

Chapter Six

Hunter bent down to examine a rusty yellow tricycle that was lying in the middle of Mango Street. *No, too mangled and a wheel missing, too,* he thought. He stood up, saw that Angerman was watching him through his battered picture frame. He gave the tricycle a swift, hard kick that sent it crashing over the curb.

"Sometimes the little kids like stuff like this," Hunter explained. "They like having lots of different bikes to ride."

Angerman didn't say anything, just lowered the picture frame and kept walking. The naked mannequin bumped along behind him, tethered to its rope. Hunter noticed for the first time how scratched up it was, how badly dented. He also noticed that Angerman had taken the maroon and blue silk tie off his head and tied it over the mannequin's mouth, like a gag.

"It's all part of the routine," Hunter went on, trying not to stare at the mannequin. "I do all the hunting for the family. I go on maneuvers, I get provisions. Of course I've had to increase the terrortory over time, since most of the houses and stores in Lazarus are pretty picked over."

"You mean overnight trips and so forth," Angerman said.

"Yes, and so forth," Hunter replied. He hadn't actually gone on an Overnight Maneuver yet. He had mastered Lazarus over the last five years, knew every street and alley and abandoned building like the back of his hand. But he hadn't quite worked himself up to going beyond its borders. A new town meant new geography to learn. New skeletons to clean up. All of it without being able to see very well. And on top of that, the thought of being away from home during one of the usual thunderstorms made him a little nervous—although as the commandment said, Don't Let a Little Rain Spoil Your Day!

But Angerman didn't need to know such details.

Hunter fingered the lens in his pocket. It shouldn't be too hard to find another pair of glasses somewhere. He used to kick them out of the way, not even realizing how important they were.

Up ahead, Action Figure was scrambling over a burned-out car that was lying belly-up on the street. He carried his new bow in his hands, and the arrows were in a makeshift quiver he had crafted out of old socks and one of Baby's discarded bonnets.

Action Figure liked following Hunter wherever he went—always had, even though he wasn't supposed to. Except these days, Action Figure didn't exactly follow. He was usually forty, fifty feet ahead, not so much leading but disappearing down this street, into that house, forcing Hunter to follow *him*.

"He your brother?" Angerman spoke up.

"Yeah," Hunter replied, wary.

"You two don't look much alike," Angerman remarked.

Hunter bristled. "He takes after—" he began, then stopped. Felt hot inside.

*A tall man with white-blond hair, green eyes, big
strapping shoulders. Catch on Saturday mornings, just
the guys, while the baby scooted around the driveway on
his tricycle, brring brring! Trying to intercept the ball:
Me play catch too, Poppy, me play!*

Hunter closed his eyes, felt like sitting down, right
there in the middle of the street. Or curling up on the
cool, cool grassy curb, under a tree.

He opened his eyes, let the blurry white brilliant
landscape wash over him. He squeezed his hands into
fists.

"What about you, you got a brother, too?" he asked
Angerman, not trying to sound friendly at all.

Something came over Angerman then. He turned
pale, and his mouth quivered a little. "No," he replied
after a moment. "No brother."

"Where're you from?" Hunter kept at him. "Where's
your family from?" He liked it that he could jar
Angerman like this. Which made no sense to him at all.

But Angerman had recovered his composure and was
glancing around, hand shielding his eyes from the
midday sun. "There a place 'round here where I could
hunt some maps?"

"You want to hunt maps?" Hunter stopped in his
tracks. Who did this guy think he was? "Listen," he said,
raising his voice. "Let's get this thing straight. *I* do all the
hunting for this family. No one else. You need something,
you gotta clear it through me. This is my town—you
can't just start hunting stuff in the stores like you're
taking over or something."

Angerman shrugged. "Whatever, it's your town, it's
your turf. I don't care. I'm not going to be here long."

Hearing this news, Hunter felt a twinge of something, like disappointment. Which made no sense at all, either. "Oh. Huh. Well, where're you planning to go?"

"Go? Go where?" Action Figure had circled behind them and was now coming up from behind, bow and arrow in hand. Stuck on the end of the arrow was a small dead bloody mouse. "Me go too," he cried out.

Angerman smiled at the boy, raised the battered picture frame to his face. "My next destination is Washington, D.C.," he said in his anchorman voice. "My objective is to find a Grown-up called President."

Dinner—such as it was—was over, and the dishes were pushed aside. Mommy's finger trailed down page 32 of *Family Health*. "Here it is. Burns." She glanced at the close-up of someone's blistery, bubbly red cheek, winced before going on to read the fine-print paragraph next to it. "Hunter, you need to hunt me something called aloe."

"Who's it for this time?" Teacher asked. "Action again?"

Mommy shook her head. "No, Angerman. He has a bad burn on his hand. Didn't say how he got it."

The three of them—Mommy, Hunter, and Teacher— were sitting in the kitchen. The plates were stacked higgledy-piggledy, real china this time, white with a delicate border of blue-green seashells. Hunter had scavenged them from a house down the street, from some First Family whose mailbox said THE JOHNSONS.

The seashell plates were streaked with brown gravy, vestiges of their feast tonight of corned beef hash. Hunter had found a can of it, a single can, which they'd split among the eight of them. The children had been so hungry, Mommy hadn't even bothered to heat the can on the grill. It had been so long since any of them had eaten meat.

Mommy turned to Hunter, half expecting him to speak. She knew he was waiting to tell them something—he'd been trying to catch her eye all through dinner, every time Angerman was busy fooling around with the little kids. Now Hunter was sitting at the edge of his chair, staring in the direction of the living room where Angerman was giving his nightly newscast to the children. "Today in Lazarus, Florida, corned beef hash began to rain from the sky," he was saying through the picture frame. Which made the girls, Action Figure, and even Teddy Bear erupt in hysterical laughter.

Hunter leaned across the table, all seriousness. "He told me today, he's going to Washington, D.C., after this," he said in a low voice. "To find some Grown-up called President."

"President!" Teacher erupted. "You mean, the President of the United States?"

Mommy started. "That's crazy," she whispered, stealing a glance at Angerman. "Washington, D.C., is really, really far away, isn't it? Besides, why would he think President is even alive?"

Just then, Angerman called out from the living room: "We interrupt this broadcast for a special news bulletin. There are still Grown-ups! I've seem some."

"He's nuts," Hunter hissed. "There's no Grown-ups anymore—everyone knows that."

"Grown-UPS, Grown-UPS," Baby repeated, climbing onto Angerman's lap. "What are Grown-ups?"

"Is that like my Grow Up on the wall?" Doll asked him.

"Grown-up, Grown-down," Teddy Bear piped up.

Mommy saw that Angerman was staring at her— *her*—through his picture frame. She frowned at him, was surprised to find herself upset at the thought of him leaving them, undertaking this perilous journey. Maybe he was even crazier than they thought.

"It's a ridiculous idea," she told him.

Angerman put his picture frame down, rose up from the couch. Baby, Doll, Action Figure, and Teddy Bear began clambering onto his now-empty seat, jockeying for the frame.

"Mine, mine, mine," Mommy heard Action Figure say. "Givum, or I'll shoot you with my arras!"

"Action!" Mommy warned him.

Dragging the naked mannequin behind him, Angerman sauntered into the kitchen. "It is not ridiculous," he told her. "I mean, don't you want to get some answers?"

"What answers?" Teacher asked him.

"Answers about what happened," Angerman said, his voice rising. He whirled around, pointed to the little ones in the living room. Baby and Doll had the picture frame between them, and were pressing their faces through the opening, cheek to cheek, shouting "Good evening!" Teddy Bear and Action Figure were watching, entranced. "Don't you all want to find some Grown-ups to take care of these kids?" Angerman demanded.

Mommy scraped her chair back and stood up, defiant. "Stop talking about Grown-ups! And besides, we're doing just fine. Just fine."

"Oh, you are, are you?" Angerman moved one step closer to her. She could feel his hot breath on her face, could feel the rage in his body, see it in his eyes. "What's your name?" he demanded.

GraceShellyMeganJessieLaurenElizabeth. She couldn't remember. "Mommy. My name is Mommy," she insisted, her voice cracking.

"No, your *real* name," Angerman pressed. "You're not a Mommy—you're, what? Fourteen? Fifteen? You're not a Grown-up, you're a kid, like me, like Teacher, like Hunter, like everyone. And what are their names? *Her* name isn't Teacher. *His* name isn't Action Figure. We used to have real names. We used to have real Mommies and real Daddies. I want to find someone to say they're sorry for what happened! We're not supposed to live like this—we're not supposed to live like animals!"

Then Angerman raised his hand in the air, the one with the terrible blistery burn on it that Mommy wanted to treat with the thing called aloe. For a second she thought he was going to hit her, and flinched.

But instead he picked Bad Guy up by the neck and slammed it into the kitchen wall, hard. One of the seashell plates clattered off the table and onto the floor, and broke into a dozen pieces.

Baby began to cry, then Doll, then Teddy Bear. Their cries filled the awful silence in the house.

Hunter stood up. "You are out of line, mister," he hissed at Angerman. Mommy noticed that Teacher was writing like mad on the back of an old Cereos box, recording everything.

Mommy glared at Angerman. "How dare you," she said. "How dare you come into our home and wreck everything like this!"

"You know I'm right," Angerman told her.

Mommy opened her mouth to say something, then clamped it shut again. She didn't want to pursue this with him, not in front of the little ones.

Who were still crying. Who needed her.

"Shh, Mommy's here. Let's go upstairs, Mommy will read you a story," she said, rushing into the living room.

There were a few faint stars in the evening sky. Teacher gazed up at them, trying to make out a constellation. She squinted, cocked her head from side to side. Nothing was coming to her—there was no order to them.

At last she turned to Angerman, who was walking in silence by her side. "So what's *your* real name?" she asked him.

Angerman shrugged. "I don't know. I don't remember."

Teacher nodded. She knew what he meant. "I don't remember, either," she said. "None of us do." She added, "I thought once that maybe my name was Virginia. But then I found this book about the United States. Virginia is a state."

"Could be a name, too," Angerman told her.

"I don't know," Teacher said.

She kicked a pebble, listened to it skitter across the pavement and *plop*, *plunk* down into the murky waters of the canal. In the distance, a panther screamed. Two bats appeared out of nowhere in pursuit of bugs, swooshed past with a crisp fluttering of wings, and then disappeared into the blue-black darkness behind the Quik-E-Mart. Night birds called from all sides.

A cool breeze stirred Teacher's hair, felt good against her face. Just then, she saw an alligator, or what looked like an alligator. It slithered out from behind the Hair-Do Beauty Shoppe and into the canal with a quiet splash. They'd have to be more alert. By long habit, Teacher picked up a few rocks, ready to throw.

She shivered, then turned to Angerman. "During the First Year, we all found each other," she said. "I was living with Teddy and some other children, but they . . . died. The other ones. They got sick, like they had colds but the colds got worse and then . . . well, they died. And then Teddy and me met Hunter and his brother, and we all found Mommy and the girls in the house we live in now. And then Teddy got sick, too, like those other kids. Coughing. But Mommy made him better because she had this book about family health, and she made Hunter hunt for medicine."

"So Teddy's your brother."

Teacher shrugged. "I don't—I don't really know. I can't remember. He was just one of the little kids I was with when the Grown-ups—you know."

"You're the only ones left in Lazarus?" Angerman asked, although it sounded more like a statement than a question.

Teacher thought about the strays, the little boy and the girl. "I thought we were the only ones left in the world," she said.

"You're not," Angerman said. "There's me. And I'm pretty sure I've seen Grown-ups in the distance when I was traveling. So I don't believe there's nobody but you guys and me in the whole world. And I'm going to find out."

Teacher kicked another pebble. "You know, we can't leave Lazarus. Our family, I mean. Because of Mommy."

Angerman glanced at her. "Why not?"

"Mommy can't leave the house," Teacher said. "Ever since . . . the Fire-us, and everything that happened. She's too afraid."

Angerman looked stunned. "You mean she hasn't left the house in five years?"

Teacher shook her head. "Not even once. So that's why . . . that's why the family has to stay."

"But you all *have* to leave," Angerman insisted, waving aside a mosquito. "You have no choice. You're running out of food. There's almost nothing left in this town."

"Going to Washington is no solution!" Teacher cried out. "It's too far. It would be too dangerous. There's alligators, and panthers . . . and, and . . ." She sucked in a breath. "There's the Fire-us. What if it's still out there somewhere? What if it kills us?" she whispered.

"It may kill us right here in Lazarus," Angerman pointed out. "It kills Grown-ups. How old are you, Teacher? You're going to be a Grown-up in a few years, too."

Teacher's eyes blazed at him. "Don't say that!"

"If there's a cure for it," Angerman said. "It's going to be in Washington. President will have information."

"What if President isn't even alive anymore?" Teacher asked him. "You could be wrong about seeing Grown-ups. We've never seen any—maybe you just thought you did. I used to think I saw a policeman at the end of our street every day. And sometimes I think I hear Grown-up people talking, but it's not real."

"President is alive," Angerman said. "I feel it. I know deep down, in my bones."

They turned the corner and walked in silence for a

while. Teacher's mind was swirling with thoughts. *What if Angerman was right? What if the only hope for their survival was leaving Lazarus, was going to Washington to find a Grown-up who might not even be alive anymore? But if there were Grown-ups, then they really should go look for them, shouldn't they?*

But how could they ever leave their house, with Mommy's condition? She got sick, hysterical just walking two feet out of the front door.

They were coming up on the house now. Teacher was glad. She was tired, tired of all this, and eager to lie down for a little while. And then get up at midnight or so to work on The Book, to search for answers to this New Question: Grown-ups, Real or Ghosts?

Just then, Teacher saw something on the front stoop. "Look!" she whispered to Angerman.

There were two little figures eating out of the ant-filled dish of ice cream cone bits that Teacher had left out. Crouched down, eating ravenously, like wild animals.

"Hey!" Angerman called out, hurrying his steps.

Teacher grabbed his arm. "No!"

But it was too late. The two little figures had heard them and scampered into the darkness. By the time Teacher and Angerman reached the house, there was no sign of them anywhere, no sign that they had even been there except for the empty overturned dish lying in the grass.

Chapter Seven

At last the sound of regular breathing came from the bed instead of the fitful, fretful sniffs and sighs. Baby and Doll were sound asleep. Mommy pushed herself up from where she sat cross-legged on the floor against the wall, and tiptoed out of the darkened room. At the door to Hunter, Teddy Bear, and Action Figure's room, she stopped and listened. Action Figure's breath came slow and regular, too.

Not that Mommy believed he was really asleep. She was pretty sure he was faking, waiting for a chance to slip outside and prowl in the darkness. Short of tying him up there was nothing they could do to control Action Figure. Warnings about beasts didn't alarm him, threats of punishment didn't frighten him, and pleas didn't move him. Sometimes Mommy wondered if he would run away and simply become a wild thing. It wouldn't surprise her to find him gone one day. She couldn't even get near him with the scissors to cut his hair. Any time she tried he growled at her and ran away.

Mommy moved down the hall to the staircase, where a soft glow of light welled up from downstairs. From where she stood, she could see the corner of a living room chair and Teacher's bony elbow jutting out and the dummy that Angerman always dragged around lying facedown on the stained carpet. Angerman's voice as he spoke to Teacher and Hunter raised the hairs on Mommy's arms, and made her ball her hands into fists.

She hated him.

At that moment, she hated him so much that she thought she would fly into fragments, hissing and acid, burning everything. The screaming spirit rose inside her like something with claws, trying to make her hurt herself.

But she forced it to go, chased it away. Scolding and stern, an angry protector. In a moment, she felt like herself again, and made her feet move, carry her down the stairs step by step toward the light.

The others looked up when she joined them in the living room.

"We're going to trap the wild ones tonight," Angerman said. Like he was in charge. Like the decision was his to make and was already settled. Who did he think he was?

Mommy sat on the sofa beside Hunter, drawing her knees up and hugging them. She stared at her bare feet, noting that she had to clip her toenails. She knew the others were waiting for her to say something, maybe to disagree with Angerman. She could feel Hunter and Teacher waiting for her. She looked up, avoiding their eyes and looking instead at Angerman. As long as they talked about catching the wild children, they didn't have to talk about leaving Lazarus.

"We just have to figure out how to do it," he continued.

Hunter shifted on the sofa. He seemed uncomfortable and on edge, and kept starting to reach for his pocket and then would draw his hand back. "We could rig a catcher thing—prop up a big box or something with a stick and bait it with food. When they go under the box to get the food, we spring the trap."

"What if an animal gets the food first?" Teacher put in. Her forehead was tight. "We can't afford to waste any."

Angerman made a quick gesture with one hand, dismissing her. "They'll be back. They have found food here, so they'll come back when the coast is clear."

"How can you be so sure? Are you an expert on wild children?" Mommy demanded. She felt ridiculous. She wanted to catch the children more than anyone, and here she was arguing about it, but she couldn't stop the words from coming. "And besides, it's dangerous at night. Animals can get them."

Angerman turned to her, leaning forward to rest his elbows on his knees while he clicked one thumbnail across his chipped tooth. "That's why we can't wait any longer," he mumbled. "They've been lucky so far, but it's only a matter of time before something gets them. We have to bring them in."

Mommy met his gaze. He was crazy. She was pretty sure he was crazy and dangerous. But he didn't seem crazy and dangerous now. Again, Hunter and Teacher were watching her, waiting for her approval. She made herself nod her head. Up and down. Once. She really hated him.

"We'll take turns keeping watch," Hunter said, standing up, almost bouncing up. Now that they were going to act, he was more himself, and he paced, his voice growing more animated. "There's a good moon tonight which will help. I know a box—there's one in the house next door, a big plastic storage bin. That'll work."

Teacher stood up, too, and reached for one of the

flashlights. "I'll see what we can use for bait."

As Hunter and Teacher were about to leave, a noise from the stairs turned everyone's head. Action Figure had crept down, and was now crouched on the bottom step, nodding. He clutched his bow before him with both hands, his knuckles white.

"I gotta bone arra, shoota panther," he said. His voice was almost hoarse with excitement. "Shoota gator orra bear."

"No, Action," Mommy began, but Hunter interrupted.

"Been practicing?" he asked his little brother.

Action Figure sprang off the step toward Hunter, all joy. "Ya, ya! I c'n help!"

Mommy glared at Hunter, but he shook his head, knowing what she was going to say. "I know, but look, there's only us, and you know, you can't—you wouldn't be able to—"

"I know." Mommy let out a harsh laugh and leaned back against the sofa cushions, dragging her hands back through her hair. "I know, I know. I'm no use. I can't go outside. I'm no use. No use."

"Action, you and me, we'll be one team," Hunter said, putting one arm around Action Figure's shoulders to stop his jiggling. "Teacher, you and Angerman can be another."

"Right," Teacher said. She didn't look at Mommy.

Angerman rubbed his hands together, and there was a gleam of something in his eyes as he stood up, kicking the mannequin aside. "Can't wait to hear the news tonight!"

——

The full moon had moved from the right side of the driveway over to the left, and a fuzzy aura surrounded it now, making it bigger and whiter in the sky and everything else blacker. Hunter and Action Figure stood at the base of the banyan tree that took up most of the side yard, its strange reaching legs stretching from the moss-draped branches down to the ground. Hunter boosted his brother up, although he hardly needed the help. Action Figure scrambled up like a monkey, and hung upside down by his knees, holding out his hands.

"Bone arra."

Hunter passed them to his brother. Then he grabbed a branch and hoisted himself up. The rope to release the trap ran up the trunk, and Hunter was careful he didn't kick it by mistake, dropping the trap over the dish of applesauce and ice cream cone bits on the front steps.

They each found a perch that gave them a good view of the front door and of the driveway. The moon's light cast a firefly glow over the sandy drive. Hunter identified landmarks by their shadows: there the arching trunk of the palm, there the twiggy, rampant oleanders, there the clump of palmettos that took over a little more turf each year. Hunter squinted, trying to put sharp edges to the things he was looking at, but he knew he was seeing them more by memory than by eyesight. He knew what they looked like, and that was the picture he saw.

Then he remembered the lens in his pocket. He took it out and held it to one eye.

He could almost hear a *click* as though he'd flicked a switch. The darkness was just as deep, but the shadows were sharper now. The hand shapes of the palmettos had separate fingers instead of just holding a fan, and the hummocks of overgrown grass were clear sprays of grass blades, not just swaying forms.

Above him, Action Figure thrashed briefly among the branches. A leaf hit Hunter on the cheek and something else, something heavy and alive—a big spider or a palmetto bug.

"Be quiet," he whispered, swatting away whatever had landed on him. "Quit fooling around with the bow. You'll scare those wild kids off."

"Gotta be ready," Action Figure said.

Hunter faced the front steps again, where the trap made a blocky shadow. They would be ready, but for what? He didn't really think the little children would come back. How could they? How could they remember their way to a strange place, such little ones? He saw, more clearly than with the magic lens, memory bits of little children in the early days after Fire-us, crying and lost, falling into swimming pools, huddled under cars during thunderstorms, gorging themselves on candy until they died, silent and staring at the white-hot sky.

He had to stop himself from crying out to Action Figure, needing to hear his brother's voice, to know the boy was safe. Frowning, he turned his head to look down the driveway. The shadows moved as the night breeze came through, and insects chirred in the undergrowth.

Two shadows moved out into the middle of the driveway.

Hunter clicked his tongue and breathed his brother's name. "Look."

Slowly, an inch at a time, Hunter pushed himself backward to the trunk, straining to keep the two shapes in sight. He groped behind himself for the rope and closed his fingers around it. The children were nearly abreast of the big banyan, and in a few more steps would reach the trap. They moved cautiously, step by step.

Above him, Hunter heard stealthy movements as Action Figure pulled himself into a better position. Then he heard a sharp hiss of Action Figure's breath. Hunter glanced back at the drive.

Another shape had separated from the shadows, long and lean, four legs and a long, swinging tail. Panther. It crouched, wriggling its rear end, ready to spring. The children were just beside the banyan.

"Shoot, Action," he gasped. "Shoot it!"

Without thought, Hunter dropped from the tree and threw himself at the children. There was a *ssssssip* and a wild snarl that filled Hunter's ears as he hit the ground, tangled among thrashing, scratching limbs.

Upstairs, Mommy bolted out of her chair. Screeching, yelling, screaming—the commotion outside set her heart hammering against her ribs. Her hands shook as she switched on her flashlight and ran out into the hall. Teacher was three steps ahead of her, and they could hear Angerman running to the front door.

"OPEN THE DOOR! OPEN THE DOOR!" That was Hunter yelling at the top of his voice. "OW!"

There was another kind of screaming, too. Two or three voices screeching and caterwauling. Mommy and Teacher raced down the stairs, their footsteps pounding and their flashlight beams bobbing ahead of them.

The door slammed against the wall as Angerman threw it open, and a confusion of bodies tumbled inside. In the scattered light it was a jumble of images: frantic eyes, flailing limbs, Hunter struggling to hold on to two dirty, ragged creatures, and outside still, hopping from foot to foot, Action Figure howling and yelping, waving his bow and arrow. "KILT IT! KILT IT! ME AN' MY BONE ARRA! KILTA PANTHER! WHOO-HOOO!"

Angerman and Teacher were trying to help Hunter subdue the small children who still struggled like wildcats. The little ones made no sounds that seemed human but snarled and hissed. Mommy knelt by Teacher, who had one of them pinned down with her whole body. Hunter and Angerman had the other one, each holding an arm and a leg.

"Here, don't hurt them," Mommy cried, trying to tuck her flashlight under her arm and put her hands out to the terrified child under Teacher. She cooed and shushed, murmuring nonsense sounds to soothe them, but Action Figure was still whooping and screeching his victory outside.

"Action, get in here! Shut the door!" she yelled.

Hunter gasped as the one he held landed a hard kick in his stomach. "Can we just let them go?" His face was scratched, and he tried to wipe a dotted line of blood off his cheek with his shoulder.

The moment the door was safely shut, everyone let go. The wild children stopped thrashing and crawled to each other, clinging. They shook and whimpered, a sound almost like a puppy's whine or a kitten's pitiful mewl. Mommy thought she would cry.

"What can we do?" Teacher asked, her arms folded tightly across her chest.

"Here, here," Mommy crooned. She held out one hand toward them, and got down on her knees. "It's all right. You're safe now."

Angerman laughed at that. "Yes, we're all perfectly safe."

"Shut up," Hunter said.

Mommy ignored them, knee-walking another step nearer the children. They stared at her, their thin, dirty faces streaked with tears. "We won't hurt you. Are you hungry? Do you want some food?" She mimed putting food in her mouth, and one of them sobbed, reaching out a grubby hand.

Teacher abruptly ran out of the front hall. They could hear her footsteps clattering as she stumbled up the stairs. Even Action Figure was shocked into silence. Mommy sniffed.

"Come with me, I have food for you," she said with a quiver in her voice.

Angerman knelt beside her and gathered one of them up into his arms. Mommy took the other. The wild children had stopped struggling, exhausted with fear. Slowly, carefully, they carried the strays into safety.

Chapter Eight

Teacher woke up to the sound of rain and of something drip, drip, dripping in her bedroom. She opened her eyes with a groan—it was such an effort to wake up, had been ever since the unsleeping sickness she had caught the First Year. She squinted and winced against the morning light. Such as it was. It was going to be a dreary day.

And then she saw it. There was a leak in the ceiling, an ominous-looking brown stain that was weeping dirty drops of water onto her desk. It took her a minute to realize that the leak was directly over the desk where she had left The Book.

Cursing, she struggled out of the tangle of bedsheets and rushed across the room, grabbing The Book. She had left it open to page 154. She had spent much of the night recording everyone's dreams, the things they had babbled in their sleep. But the water from the leak had bled the purple ink, erased a bunch of words, run sentences together:

> PLEASE DON'T PLEASE DON'T LEAVE ME
> I HAVE NO LEGS PANTHER COME
> WITH ME I HAVE FOOD FOR YOU

Teacher swayed for a second. Oh, yes, *them*. She remembered them now, their dirt-covered faces, their hysterical crying. Their thin, thin bodies, thinner than any of them, even.

Those strays had been so hungry, she supposed Mommy had fed them the rest of the ice cream cones or whatever. Teacher hadn't stuck around to find out. In any case, it probably meant that there wouldn't be any food for breakfast. Hunter would have to make an emergency expedition. She'd tell him to add glue to the list, for The Book, and batteries for the flashlights. And something for the leak, which was making the plaster ceiling buckle and sag. Everything—*everything*—was falling apart around here, she thought with a swift surge of panic.

Teacher blew on the damp page of The Book and set it down on her bed. And then got dressed in her faded sundress and padded down the stairs.

She heard quiet, earnest eating noises from the kitchen. Peering in, she saw Mommy sitting at the table with the two of them. A boy and a girl, Teacher could definitely see that now. They were smaller than Baby and Doll and Teddy Bear and Action Figure. Maybe five or six or something like that.

Mommy was feeding them bits of orange—first the girl, then the boy, then the girl again. Mommy only had one orange, and she kept breaking the sections smaller and smaller in order to stretch it out. Teacher didn't know where Mommy had even gotten that one orange— she must have been saving it from one of Hunter's recent expeditions for an emergency.

Teacher gave a little cough, then walked into the kitchen. The strays sat up in their chairs and stared at her, their brown eyes wide and alarmed. Ready to bolt. The juice from the orange dribbled down their chins, streaked the dirt on their faces.

"They need washing," Teacher observed. "They're filthy."

"I haven't had a chance yet," Mommy replied with a sigh. "They won't hardly let me touch them."

"Where'd they sleep?" Teacher asked.

Mommy broke off another bit of orange and handed it to the boy. He grabbed it with his grubby fingers and devoured it, but his eyes were still fixed on Teacher.

"I tried to put them in bed with the girls and me, but they just wriggled out," Mommy explained. "I found them under the bed this morning. They both peed in their pants, but I managed to take their shorts off before they woke up."

Teacher glanced down, saw that the strays were wearing nothing but their dirty T-shirts from last night. "What's your name?" she asked the boy. Silence. "What's *your* name?" she said, turning to the girl. Silence again.

She frowned, and crossed the kitchen to where she had left a bucket of rainwater on the counter the other day. She brought it over to the table, along with a couple of the pale-blue *RFB* napkins. She couldn't stand dirt.

Seeing the bucket, the boy and the girl whimpered and tried to scramble from their chairs. Whereupon Mommy put her hands on their shoulders—or rather, just above them—and smiled, and said in her gentlest Mommy voice, "It's okay, that's Teacher, she won't hurt you."

The strays hesitated. Teacher scooted a chair close to the boy, sat down with the bucket and napkins, leaned forward. The acrid smell of urine greeted her nostrils, and she had to stifle a groan of disgust.

She dipped one of the *RFB* napkins into the rainwater, then reached toward the boy's grimy cheek. He flinched when she touched him, let out a low growl like a dog.

"Don't fight me, all right?" Teacher murmured, grasping his arm to hold him still. "You'll feel better when you're clean." She noticed that the boy had a light smattering of peach-colored freckles across his nose. And gold flecks in his brown eyes, like sunlight on river water.

One cheek done. Good.

"Angerman's right, y'know," Teacher said to Mommy as she started on the other cheek.

Mommy took the other *RFB* napkin and scooted close to the girl. "About what?" she said, a shade too shrill.

"We can't stay here," Teacher said. "There's no more food."

But Mommy just ignored her. She dipped the napkin into the rainwater and began dabbing at the girl's forehead. "You're just little things, aren't you? Just babies," she cooed. "Where'd you come from? Who was taking care of you?"

The girl squirmed against the napkin, then let out a loud, protesting meow.

"Thinks she's a cat or something," Teacher said.

"Still hungry?" Mommy asked the girl.

The girl just meowed again. Mommy turned, frowned at Teacher. "Something—there's something wrong with them," she whispered. "They don't know how to talk?"

The boy began whimpering, then barking. Teacher felt something warm and wet on her feet. Glancing down, she realized that the boy had just peed all over the floor.

"Ugh, this thing needs housebreaking!" Teacher cried out. She scraped her chair back, began swiping at her feet with the napkin.

The boy stared at her, eyes enormous, and continued to bark and yip. The girl continued meowing.

Just then, Baby, Doll, and Teddy Bear came marching into the kitchen, dressed in matching stained white slips that hung to their ankles. Long strands of Christmas tinsel were wrapped around their necks. Seeing the boy and girl, who were still barking and meowing, Baby let out a loud, happy shriek and, clapping her hands, cried out, "Can we keep them? Please, Mommy, can we?"

The shelves of Jim's Army and Navy store were practically untouched. Hunter had never been able to hunt for supplies inside, because the windows had bars on them, and the front door had been barricaded by a fallen tree. But now, he and Angerman together had been able to shift the tree trunk enough to get the door open.

There was no need for a flashlight as they made their way through the store. Part of the roof was gone, had collapsed from repeated storm damage. The sound of rain falling and dripping through the opening mingled with the sounds of the boys' footsteps and of Bad Guy clunking, scraping along on his tether behind Angerman. The guy never let that mannequin out of his sight, no matter what.

"Lamps, kerosene, waterproof matches," Angerman called out. He stuffed the items into an olive-green nylon sack that he had procured from aisle 4. The label was still shiny and glossy, with a picture of some smiling First

Family on a camping trip. "Swiss Army knife. Hey, why not, let's take a couple."

Hunter didn't reply. He watched as Angerman took one of the knives, flicked open the blade, swished it through the air in a series of rapid arcs.

Then Angerman turned around and pointed the blade at Bad Guy's head. "What, you gonna turn us in, Pig?" he spat. "You *gonna*?"

"There's tents in this aisle over here," Hunter said. Angerman made him nervous. Hunter was still convinced that there was something dangerous, unbalanced about him. Obviously, he needed to be reined in. "Let's get this over with, okay? Weather might take a turn for the worse, and the girls are expecting us to bring home dinner."

"Dinner! Let's go to aisle 5, folks!" Angerman threw the Swiss Army knives into his sack, then went around the corner. Hunter frowned and followed.

Angerman paused at the beginning of aisle 5, reached for a couple of packages, and turned them over in his hand. Hunter leaned forward, squinted, read the label.

Dried beef.

Dried beef! Hunter's mouth dropped open. There were boxes and boxes of the stuff—chili and dried soups and instant pudding and all kinds of things—enough to feed them all for weeks.

Just then, he heard light footsteps behind them, barely audible even on the damp, moldy carpeting. He whirled around. His brother had snuck up on him and Angerman, was hiding behind a stack of cardboard boxes labeled WATER PURIFIERS. Hunter could just make out the top of his sun-bleached head, which was matted thickly with thistles and dead leaves.

"Action, what're you doing here?" Hunter demanded.

Action Figure stepped out from behind the boxes, a sly grin on his face. He was dressed in his usual denim cutoffs and boots, and he bore his bow and arrow. His bare chest and thin, sinewy arms were wet and goose bumpy from the rain.

"Lookin for dead panther," Action said. "Kilt it last night with my bone arra! Bring it home ta skin an eat!"

Hunter clasped the boy's shoulder. He remembered his first hunt, or his first attempt at a hunt, thinking he had killed a small deer for the family to eat. In the First Year.

"Look. It's probably not dead—I bet you just wounded it. That's not a very strong bow," he lied, not wanting to say his brother wasn't as strong as he thought he was.

Action Figure raised his chin. "Kilt it!" he insisted.

"*I'll* help you find your dead panther, Action," Angerman offered, "as soon as I finish hunting for supplies here."

Hunter bristled. Angerman shouldn't be encouraging his brother like this. It was a waste of time, the panther couldn't possibly be dead, and besides, it was crazy dangerous to go after a wounded animal. He *was* nuts.

But before Hunter had a chance to say anything, Action had stepped around him, and was gazing up at Angerman. "Supplies? Fer what?"

"For my trip to Washington, my man," Angerman replied. He held up a long red bungee cord, inspected it.

Then lowered it wriggling and writhing into his sack, as if it were a snake.

Action Figure guffawed and pounded his chest. "Me go to Wash'ton, too!" he announced without even a look at Hunter.

"What?" Hunter cried out.

Then he turned away, rubbing his eyes with a calloused hand. They were tired. *He* was tired. He was tired of trying to figure out what to do about this Washington business. Because as much as he hated to admit it, Angerman was right. The family couldn't stay in Lazarus much longer. No one was coming to rescue them. He had painted big letters on the highway in that first year, wrote WE'RE STILL HERE big enough for anybody in an airplane to see—if there were still airplanes. But nothing flew across the sky but birds, and no one was coming to Lazarus to take care of them.

And yet there was no way they could leave, either.

"We can't go to Washington," Hunter told his brother.

"You kint stop me," Action Figure replied. "Me go with Angerman!"

Hunter balled up his fists, resisted the white-hot rage that rose within him and made him want to knock Angerman against the shelves and pummel him. "Can't you just stay here? Can't you just stay here and help us take care of the children?" he said, trying to keep his voice level. "We've got plenty of food, now."

Angerman laughed. "Look. I'm leaving. You can go with me or not, but I'm leaving, and I'm not coming back."

Then he turned and continued down aisle 5,

dragging his nylon sack and Bad Guy behind him. Action Figure skipped behind him. "Me bring bone arra to Wash'ton. Shoot panthers! Shoot Presda!"

Hunter sighed and followed. Listening to his brother and Angerman chattering about panthers, weapons, water bottles, provisions, he couldn't help but feel a small, secret thrill of excitement, too. A journey to Washington! It would be the ultimate hunting expedition.

But there was no way it could ever happen. Because Mommy could never leave. And there was no way he, Hunter, could ever leave Mommy behind.

By evening, the rain had stopped. Teacher sat at her desk, chewing on her pencil that said PAIN-FREE DENTISTRY! CALL 555-1234. With her other hand she twisted a strand of her hair around and around one finger, and then pulled gently, gently, then very hard, until it hurt.

Cursing, muttering to herself, she let go of her hair and began to write. On page 34, over an old brochure with a picture of a big white fancy house and the words *our nation's capital:*

> What are we gonna do? It's my job to figure
> it out and get the Answers for everyone.
> There's almost no food left in Lazarus. Plus
> now we have those strays Puppy and Kitty to
> feed. Angerman's leaving for Washington
> soon, and we should go with him except we
> can't because on account of Mommy not
> being able to go outside. Not even the yard—

how can she go all the way to Washington, wherever that is? Besides, the trip could be dangerous, with alligators and panthers and everything. And the Fire-us, there's always the Fire-us. But it could be dangerous here, too, if we stay. We need Answers.

She underlined the word *Answers* five times with her Pain-Free Dentistry pencil.

The sounds of barking and meowing interrupted her, made her glance up from The Book. Puppy and Kitty were standing in the doorway, each clinging to one of Angerman's pant legs. Teacher noticed that he had gotten new tan and black clothes at the army and navy store. They were spotted like leaves.

The two children actually looked happy. Or, at least, not totally miserable and terrified. "What'd you do to them?" Teacher asked Angerman, surprised.

Angerman shrugged. "What? Nothing. Listen, we came to use the Grow Up."

Teacher raised one eyebrow. What did Angerman care how old the strays were? "Oh."

She watched as Angerman positioned Puppy and Kitty side by side against the frame of her door. She noted that both strays looked much better than they had last night or even this morning at breakfast.

Mommy and Teacher had managed to clean them up and put some of the kids' clothes on them. A yellow T-shirt and shorts for him, and a pink sundress for her. They looked almost human.

They still hadn't said a word, not real human words—just continued with their barking and meowing.

Baby and Doll had named them Puppy and Kitty and the names had stuck.

"How old d'you think they are?" Teacher asked Angerman, who was trying to keep the strays very still against the doorframe.

Angerman didn't reply. He was frowning at the Grow Up.

When he didn't reply, Teacher tucked her pencil behind one ear, scooted her chair back, and joined him and the strays at the door.

The top of Puppy's head—still dirty and tangly, since he wouldn't let Mommy or Teacher shampoo his hair—reached the mark that said *April 2, 1996: 5 years old.* Kitty's head was just shy of it.

"Yeah, that seems right," Teacher said, nodding. "They could be five." She glanced up at Angerman. "Which means they would have been born—"

But Angerman had turned away and was stomping down the hall, muttering under his breath. His fists were clenched into tight balls. Puppy and Kitty bounded after him, barking and meowing.

"In the Year of Fire-us," Teacher called after them. But Angerman didn't turn around and neither did the strays.

"In the Year of Fire-us," Teacher repeated to herself. What did that mean?

She extracted the Pain-Free Dentistry pencil from behind her ear and returned to her desk. Then she began writing again in The Book.

Chapter Nine

Mommy was sure he was completely nuts, but he was leaving, and it didn't matter anymore how crazy he was. Good riddance. Get lost. See you later—way, way later. Don't hurry back now. Go on your insane wild-goose chase.

She sat at the dining-room table, trying to make a hunting list: toothpaste, more vitamins, tweezers. But every time she heard the sound of Angerman's bustling movements behind her, her attention flew into the living room. She heard Angerman mutter something to Bad Guy, heard him call the mannequin a dirty word, and she flinched.

"Hey, watch your mouth, okay?"

"Sorry!"

There was no use pretending anymore that she wasn't paying attention to him. Mommy turned around in her chair and surveyed the chaos behind her in the other room.

It looked as though Angerman had raided a camping supply store and dumped everything onto the living room floor: nesting cookware, matches, batteries and lanterns, a folding saw, a black plastic bag with a hose at one end and SOLAR SHOWER written in white lettering across the top, a collapsible cup, a blow-up sleeping pad and a sleeping bag stuffed tight into a bright blue sack, a tent bundled in another slippery fabric bag, an orange backpack with buckles and mesh pockets and zippers all over it. Angerman was sorting his gear in front of a rapt audience. Doll, Baby, and Teddy Bear sat on the sofa, watching him in breathless silence, while the two tiny ones—Puppy and Kitty—crouched on the floor together below the chair where Bad Guy was propped upright. The mannequin had a strip of tape over its mouth like a gag.

The back door banged, and there was a squeaky, trundling commotion. Action Figure fought his way through the doorway, dragging a child's red metal wagon. It was their water wagon. "Put stuffin this," he said, a triumphant grin on his dirty face.

"Perfect," Angerman replied. "Put all this dried food on it, kid."

Mommy looked back across the dining-room table. Hunter sat across from her, his head in his hands, staring at nothing. Mommy could tell he was trying not to cry.

"Hey, you guys remember when the cars worked?" Angerman asked, raising his voice. "Wasn't that great?"

"Don't amember it," Action Figure said. He squatted among the camping equipment, pawing through the freeze-dried food and puzzling over the cooking directions.

Hunter nodded but still didn't look up. "I do." He cleared his throat. "So. You're leaving first thing tomorrow?"

"Bright and early!" Angerman sang out. "The call of the open road, the horizon is my destination, boys and girls, behind the wheel of my Oldsmobile. Got an appointment with destiny."

Mommy flipped her notepad to a new page. *We won't let him take Action. Don't worry*, she wrote, and slid it across the table to Hunter.

"Well, good luck on your journey," she said over her shoulder to Angerman.

Baby slid off the sofa and stepped over the piles to Angerman. She was pouting. "Does this mean we don't get to hear the news no more?"

"Oh, hey." Angerman sat back on his heels and took Baby's hand. "The news is mostly bad, Baby—you won't miss it."

"We will!" Doll said, her voice rising to a wail.

"Okay, okay, okay," Angerman said. He reached for his picture frame, which was buried beneath a carton labeled CANTEENS.

The moment he held the picture frame to his face, Angerman slipped into his broadcasting mode, complete with grown-up voice and fakey smile. "Good evening. Today's top story: negotiations between Palestine and Israel have broken down again, leading some analysts to believe that Jerusalem will soon be threatened with skirmishing in the streets. In a related story, Christian Fundamentalists picketed outside the White House today, demanding that any issue of control of this holy city take Christian believers into account and urging the presence of armed Christian troops as a safety measure."

The young ones gaped at him, their faces blank. Angerman looked down, as though reviewing his notes. Then he flashed a bright smile. "In further news, authorities announced today that the wild children known as Puppy and Kitty have won an all-expenses-paid trip to Washington to see President."

"No!" Mommy shoved her chair back and leaped to her feet. Three long strides and she was standing in front of Angerman, shielding Puppy and Kitty from him. "They are not going anywhere!"

Angerman tossed his frame aside and shrugged. "Shows what you know, Mommy-mommy-mommy, who isn't a mommy at all. What's her name, I wonder, what's her name? Not Mommy, no, can't be Mommy, that's not a name—she's only a kid. Laura-Susan-Maggie-Tiffany-Beth-Ramona-Vicky?"

Waves of hot and cold washed through Mommy's blood—burning, freezing, burning. He was just sitting there, cross-legged on the floor, going back to his packing while he taunted her. Mommy stared down at him, wanting to kick his face in. She whirled around and grabbed Puppy and Kitty by their hands. They rose obediently and let her march them over to the sofa, where they settled in beside Teddy Bear. The boy was sucking his thumb, his eyes darting here and there, looking for Teacher.

Mommy kneeled in front of the sofa, patting the children on their knees, trying to calm herself down. "These children have been living wild for who knows how long," she said in a tight voice. "They need rest, they need shelter, they need someone to take care of them."

"They're in danger."

Mommy looked back at him with a gasp of astonishment. "You don't get it, do you? They're *out* of danger now. I'm going to look after them. If they go off on this idiotic trip of yours they'll end up attacked by panthers or eaten by alligators!"

A whimper of fear from Teddy Bear broke into her

rage. She drew a shaky breath. "I'm sorry, Teddy. I didn't mean that. Nobody's going to get hurt by an alligator. Puppy and Kitty are staying here with us where they're safe."

Angerman stood up, brushing lint off his pants. "Oh, I have to disagree with you there, Mommy." He made a clicking sound with his tongue and held out his hands to the wild children. "Here, kitty-kitty. Come on, pup. Come on, boy."

To Mommy's horror, Puppy and Kitty clambered down from the couch and hurried to Angerman's side. They took his hands and turned their faces up to look at him. They showed no fear.

"You can't do this," Mommy said.

"Yes, I can. I am doing this." Angerman picked up Kitty and set her in the wagon, then plopped Puppy in beside her. "There. Travel in style. Go with God. Bon voyage."

"I can pullem," Action Figure piped up.

"You want to come, don't you?" Angerman asked the wild children.

They both nodded, and a shy smile broke over each face.

Mommy slumped down onto the floor, her back scraping against the edge of the sofa. He couldn't take them. He wouldn't take them. It wouldn't happen that way. When morning came they wouldn't really go with him. He would leave. He would leave by himself, the way he came, dragging his horrible Bad Guy behind him, and they'd all stay just the way they used to be but with Puppy and Kitty, too. She turned her head, and her neck seemed to creak with rust. Slowly she turned it one way and then another, shaking it slowly, slowly so that she wouldn't break.

The pool of light from the battery lamp left deep shadows in the corners of Teacher's room. She sat at her desk, her bare feet hooked over the rung of the chair, and turned the pages of The Book one by one. Her mind was loose, light, unfocused, her thoughts skimming the surfaces, touching down like a dragonfly and moving on again. She held a pencil in one slack hand. It made faint marks as it touched down in tandem with her thoughts.

Beside an ad for cat litter: a pencil mark.

Beside a page torn from a puppy care manual: a mark.

Beside a headline reading *Second Chance Saturday*: another mark.

Beside an ad that trumpeted *Coming Soon to a Theater Near You!*: a mark.

Teacher let the pencil fall from her hand. It clacked onto the desk, bouncing on the eraser end even though it was hard and dry and only left pink smudges on paper. The pencil rattled as it rolled to the edge of the desk and fell into shadow.

Those children, those wild children they had caught, they were sleeping downstairs in the living room with Angerman even now. Teacher thought she could remember that that's what you did with puppies and kittens, they slept downstairs, with a pile of rags and some newspapers nearby, and a dish of water. That was right, that's what you did. And they had made a connection to Angerman—they wanted to be with him, they followed at his heels.

Her gaze moved from the vacant space before her to the doorframe, where the Grow Up was just visible at the limit of the light. Five years old, born in the year of Fire-us. Who had taken care of little babies in that bad time? Without quite realizing it, Teacher had spread her hands out across the open Book, as though trying to absorb something from the thick layers of paper and glue. She pressed down, wanting, wanting.

Sometimes there were heavy fogs, fogs so dense that stepping off the end of the driveway onto the street would be like leaving the planet. Teacher had become lost one day in the fog, moving like a sleepwalker with her hands stretched out in front of her. She had been blinded by the fog, blind and deaf, too, because there were no sounds except drippings and tricklings, the sounds of a water world. How long she was lost she wasn't sure, but in time the fog lifted, and things became distinct, gaining shape through the trails of mist. And there, draped among the rank foliage at the edge of the street were spiderwebs, and each drooping filament was beaded with a drop of water. Teacher had stood there, staring, and saw there were dozens of spiderwebs, spiderwebs everywhere. Who could know there would be so many?—they were invisible most of the time. But the fog had come to make everything invisible and then as it lifted there were the spiderwebs, visible for the first time.

So Teacher had stood staring at the spiderwebs with the same attention she gave to anything written on paper. It was a sign. It had meaning. Only she didn't know what it was. Was it danger? Should she be frightened of them?

Pressing her hands onto The Book felt that way. She

frowned at the spread pages and reached down for the pencil. Her hand brushed the paper, as though trying to clear it of mist. Then she put her pencil on *Second*, and circled it heavily, dragged the pencil to *Coming* and circled it, too. It was a spiderweb.

What did it mean?

Teacher closed The Book, and switched off the lantern. She paused, letting the bright glow leave her eyes until she could see her way to her bed. She tucked the bulky scrapbook under her pillow, lay down, and prayed for a dream.

When it was light enough to see the outline of the palm tree through the window, Hunter sat up in bed. The upper bed of the bunks across the room was empty, but he already knew that. He had heard Action Figure leave in the middle of the night, creeping downstairs, dragging his bow and arrows behind him. Hunter had been awake ever since. In the lower bunk, Teddy Bear was balled up in sleep, sucking his thumb.

Mommy was so sure they could stop Action Figure from going with Angerman, but Hunter knew better. He knew his brother had left them a long time ago, was just waiting for the right moment to make it obvious, and a sorrow so deep it felt like dying filled Hunter's chest. He would have to watch his brother follow Angerman today, out the door, out of town, out of this life, maybe. And there wouldn't be anything Hunter could do about it. He thought probably he would never see his brother again.

Because Hunter couldn't leave. How could he, when Mommy and Teacher and the little ones needed him? How long would they survive if he just said, "Okay, bye.

I'm going now." Nobody to hunt for them, especially now when hunting was getting harder and harder. Mommy couldn't leave the house, so Teacher would have to do it, and then who would look after The Book and remember all the things about them? Teacher and The Book were what helped them remember what being real was.

His legs felt heavy as he swung them around and pushed himself up. Faint noises were already coming from downstairs: a sleep-scratchy voice, a soft kitten mewl. Metal clanked, and someone said, *"Shhh."*

Hunter plodded down the stairs to the living room entrance, and stood watching them. Action Figure glanced his way and then turned his back, busy cramming some kind of silvery mesh fabric into a plastic box. Angerman was tying Bad Guy to the orange backpack with braided rope. Puppy and Kitty sat in the wagon, surrounded by packets of freeze-dried food, watching the preparations from under a blanket.

"We're about ready," Angerman said. "I want to get an early start."

"I think you should wait for the others to wake up." Hunter tried not to look at his brother. "At least say good-bye to them."

Angerman hoisted up the backpack and swung it behind himself, hitching his arms through. He shook his head as he buckled the hip belt. "No time, no time."

"Angerman! Action, wait!" Hunter turned and dashed up the stairs, his feet thudding. "Mommy, Teacher! Wake up! They're leaving!"

"What? Now?" Mommy came stumbling out of her bedroom, blinking.

Hunter's breath was coming in harsh gasps but not

from running up the stairs. "They're leaving. They're leaving now. They're not going to say good-bye—they're just going to leave."

Mommy pushed past him, heading for the stairs in a swirl of nightgown and tangled hair. Teacher came out of her room, still dressed in the faded sleeveless dress she'd been wearing for days. Her face was haggard. Without a word, she stepped past Hunter and followed Mommy down the stairs. Hunter stood in the hallway, looking at the crayon scrawls that Baby and Doll had drawn over the walls. He would have to make himself go down there again. He would have to make himself watch Action Figure leave.

Swallowing the hard lump in his throat, he went back downstairs.

They were all in the front hallway: Angerman with Action Figure, and Mommy clutching Puppy and Kitty by their hands, and Teacher standing to one side, biting her fingernails.

"You're not taking these children," Mommy said through gritted teeth. "You don't know how to take care of them—you're crazy."

Angerman had the door open, and sun was finding its way through the dense tangle of trees and vines and bushes that crowded the house. He was maneuvering the wagon out the door, his pack—with Bad Guy strapped to it—hindering him as he bumped around in the doorway with his gear. He ignored Mommy.

"Action, don't leave," Teacher called.

Action Figure looked at Teacher as though he didn't even recognize her, as though he didn't understand what language she was speaking. He shrugged and slung his bow around one shoulder. Angerman finally got everything out the door, and the wheels of the wagon pointing out the driveway. He shook out the blanket, and folded it, making a cushion. Then he snapped his fingers.

"Come."

Puppy and Kitty tried to pick Mommy's fingers off their wrists, and when she wouldn't let go, they began to struggle, whining and whimpering with alarm.

"Stop it," Mommy said, shaking them. "You're not going with him."

At once, the two wild children began thrashing and yanking in her grip, their eyes bugging as they watched Angerman. Angerman stood in a beam of sunlight that lit his long curling hair from behind like fire. He just waited. Action Figure was already out on the driveway, kicking the air and chopping imaginary enemies with his hands. Hunter felt sick.

Puppy and Kitty wriggled and scratched at Mommy, and Puppy bent his head to bite her hand.

"Hunter!" Mommy shouted. "Ow! Help me!"

Hunter couldn't move. He felt as though he had turned to stone. But he could see. He saw Teacher step forward and begin pulling Mommy's hand away from Kitty's arm. The stringy muscles in her arms tightened as she broke Mommy's grip.

"What are you doing?" Mommy said, beginning to cry. "What are you doing? Teacher, no!"

"Let them go," Teacher said, setting Kitty loose. "They need to be with Angerman."

Kitty ran out the door to Angerman, but Mommy just gripped Puppy with both hands now, instead of only one.

She clutched him to herself, sobbing, while Teacher hooked her arms through Mommy's and dragged Mommy away from the little boy. "No, no!"

At last, Teacher pulled back far enough on Mommy's elbows for Puppy to escape. He stumbled outside and huddled beside Angerman.

"Lessgo lessgo," Action Figure chanted.

A horrible sound, a groan of pain, tore out of Mommy as she threw herself out the door after the wild children. Hunter and Teacher stood transfixed in the hallway, seeing the impossible: Mommy outside the house. She was a wreck, crying and shaking and trying to hold the children. But she was talking, too.

"I'll go with you," she cried. "I'll go with you."

Hunter began to cry, too, but he thought he was happy. He wiped his nose on the back of his hand, his eyes on his brother. "We'll all go, okay?" Teacher was nodding, and Hunter gasped again, "We'll all go."

Chapter Ten

During the First Year, when those other children she and Teddy Bear had been living with died, Teacher had wandered outside in the middle of the night with Teddy Bear asleep in her arms. She had thought about burying the dead children, but couldn't bear to do it somehow, and so she had just left them in their beds, in their white cotton pajamas that smelled of throw-up and peanut butter. She had mumbled a quick prayer—something about ashes, something about resting in peace—and then stumbled out the door into the cool, damp night that was full of the howling of dogs. She stumbled for hours in her thin nightgown and her bare, blistered feet when the sun came up. She thought, *This is it, we're all alone now, we're going to die next.*

And then, somehow, she had stumbled upon Hunter and Action Figure, camping out in the garage of Miguel's Car Repair. Hunter had been nine then—Action Figure, maybe two or three, about the same as Teddy Bear. Action Figure had been asleep, curled up on top of an old tire, sucking on an oily rag. Hunter had almost nailed Teacher with a jack when she showed up at the door. He had thought she was a coyote or an alligator or something.

Several weeks later, the four of them had found Mommy and the girls camped out in the house—*their* house. Mommy had told them that she couldn't remember how she and the little girls had ended up there. But it was comfortable, and there were plenty of beds and lots of food in the pantry. Mommy had asked Teacher and the boys to stay and live with them.

And so they became a family, the seven of them. But even then, even during their first year all together, Teacher never saw Mommy set foot outside the door. She knew—from the things Mommy moaned in her sleep almost nightly and which Teacher recorded meticulously in The Book—that Mommy was terrified, out-of-her-mind-terrified, of the outdoors. Had been ever since Fire-us took her First Mommy and First Daddy and everyone else away from her. The outdoors meant Out-of-Control, Sickness, Death.

And now Teacher was witnessing it. Mommy outdoors. In the vine-tangled front yard, Mommy was clutching at the strays as though her life depended on them. Her whole body was shaking with hysterical sobs, and every few seconds she would make a horrible gagging sound, as though she couldn't breathe.

Angerman was just standing there watching Mommy, his arms crossed over his chest. What was wrong with him, why wasn't he helping her? Teacher wondered. Action Figure was all the way to the sidewalk, his back to Mommy and the rest of them, his bow and arrow pointed at a distant flock of seagulls that was sweeping through the morning sky.

Teacher was about to go to Mommy when Hunter rushed past her and got to Mommy first. He caught Mommy by the shoulders just as she stumbled away from the strays, doubled over, and threw up into the grass.

"Are you all right—are you okay?" Hunter murmured. He bent over and stroked Mommy's tangled hair.

"I'll—be—fine," Mommy croaked. Then she hugged her stomach and threw up again. The smell reminded Teacher of those other children from long ago.

"News flash. You're not going to be able to come with us," Angerman announced to Mommy.

Hunter's head snapped up. "What're you talking about? You're not in charge here."

"Actually, I am," Angerman said. "This is my trip, and it's by invitation only. As much as I hate to be rude, I've gotta disinvite you, Mommy dearest. Can't have people who are going to be, you know, slowing the rest of us able-bodied adventurers down."

Mommy swiped a hand across her mouth and glared at him with tear-filled bloodshot eyes. "I can *do* it."

"She says she can do it," Hunter insisted. But he didn't sound very sure at all.

"I know." Teacher's mind flashed to a page in The Book, to an ad for a Coming-Soon-to-a-Theater-Near-You called *Westward Ho!* "How 'bout if we rig up some sort of cover for one of the wagons? Mommy could travel in it. That way, you know, it would be like a little traveling house. Like she wasn't outside at all."

"I think I've seen something like that at the bike shop downtown," Hunter said. "Let me go check it out."

Teacher nodded. Things were starting to fall into place now. "Good, Hunter. Why don't you take Action with you? Also, with all of us going, we'll need more stuff. I'll go inside, make a list. Angerman and I can help hunt, and maybe Teddy and Baby and Doll and the strays could pick out their favorite things they want to take with them."

"Yes, okay, fine," Angerman muttered. Teacher could tell that he wasn't too happy. Well, too bad. He had to be logical about this. It would be best if they all went together. No matter what he thought, there was no way he and Action Figure could take care of those freaky strays by themselves. And if they were all going to go, that meant he had to compromise and make concessions for Mommy's sake. It also meant they had to delay the trip for a few hours, maybe even a day, to hunt for more supplies and provisions. It was important to do these things right, to do these things in a thorough, orderly way.

As though she knew all about trips, all about traveling.

Next stop Baltimore, be sure to check for your belongings in the overhead compartment and under the seat in front of you.

Mommy was staggering, stumbling into the house, her face pale as sand. Hunter was helping her, his hand on her elbow. Murmuring little assurances. "You're going to be okay, you're going to be okay," he was saying to her as she coughed and choked back more tears.

Teacher followed them, her mind already checking off all the things she had to do.

Moonlight pooled in the driveway, made the metal on the bicycles gleam silver white. Hunter surveyed the fleet. Angerman's in front, black with taped-up handlebars. Hunter's and Action Figure's, both olive green. A blue one for Teacher, a red one for Teddy Bear, and matching pink ones for the girls. They were all brand-new bikes, not the same rusty ones they'd been riding since the last horrorcane.

They would be heading out first thing tomorrow. That is, if Hunter could figure out how to rig the double bike wagons to the backs of the older kids' bikes. He and Action Figure had hunted three of them that morning, at Cyclemania: one for Mommy, one for Puppy and Kitty, and one for lugging supplies. The problem was, how to attach them to his bike and Angerman's and Teacher's.

Hunter was also not sure how much weight the wagons could hold. Or how much weight he and Angerman and Teacher could pull, for that matter, especially over a long distance. The label on the wagons had a picture of a First Mommy pulling a baby in the seat of the cart. Mommy was thin as a stick, but she still weighed a lot more than a baby. For that matter, so did the wild children, and so did probably all their food, water, and camping gear.

Hunter hunkered down in front of one of the wagons, squinted at the gleaming metal bars and hooks and screws. It was hard, too hard, to see what he was doing in the dark. There was an instruction manual, but the print was so tiny and some of the sentences didn't really make sense. The directions were so complicated. What was he going to do? If he didn't figure it out by morning, Angerman might leave without them, after all. Angerman and Action Figure.

He heard the front screen door creak open and shut. He glanced up. Angerman was standing there, hands on hips.

"Howzit going, dude?" Angerman asked him.

Hunter stood up. "Okay. I just need to figure out how

to deal with these stupid covered wagons."

"What does the good book say?" Angerman asked him, nodding at the manual.

Hunter shrugged, handed the instructions to Angerman. "These things are always written by morons, anyway. Maybe Teacher can make sense of it."

"Let me take a crack at it," Angerman offered.

Angerman flipped to the first page. Hunter knelt down, grabbed a socket wrench that was lying on the ground, pretended to fuss with the back wheel of his brother's bike. The sound of Mommy's voice came drifting through an open window. "Pajamas, children, and brush teeth!" It was like any other night, Hunter thought. You would never know that Mommy was putting the little ones to bed in their house for the very last time. He wondered for a moment where Action Figure was. Probably not brushing his teeth. Probably outside somewhere, looking for the wounded panther.

Angerman pawed through some supplies that were piled up on a blue plastic tarp. He pulled out a pencil-thin flashlight and pointed it at the manual. "Hmm, okay, that's better. Step One. Attach Part A to Part B as shown in Diagram One. Step Two. Secure attachment with Part C as shown in Diagram Two. Head bone connected to the neck bone. Yada, yada, yada. All righty, I think I've got this. Hunter, lemme see that wrench."

Hunter gave him the wrench. "Here, hold this for me so I can see it," Angerman instructed, handing Hunter the manual and flashlight. Hunter didn't protest, just did as Angerman asked.

For the first time that evening Hunter breathed, relaxed. He could feel tension melting from his shoulders, like the wagons would get attached, like the trip was happening after all. He had to admit, the guy was good with tools. Efficient, fast, didn't get easily frustrated.

A cloud drifted across the moon. Hunter angled the flashlight, pointed the end of it way up so Angerman could see the manual better.

"Soooooo, Hunter," Angerman said, picking up a small metal bolt. "You sure were quick to come to Mommy's rescue this morning, weren't you? I still think it's a mistake, bringing her along."

Hunter felt his shoulders going all tense again. "She'll be fine. Besides, if she stays, Teacher and I'll have to stay, too. And Baby and Doll and Teddy. It'd break the family up."

"Oh, yes, the *family*," Angerman said. "The sacred all-mighty nuclear *family*." He positioned the metal bolt on the wagon's shaft and began hammering at it with the bottom of a camping skillet. "Still. I suppose it's best you all come along. I need help looking after Pup-Pup and Kitty-Kitty."

This, *this* was the part that didn't add up, Hunter thought. This guy with the sicko mannequin routine and the anchorman routine and the rage-insubordination-bad-attitude routine, wanting to bring two wild five-year-olds with him to Washington. He just didn't seem like the Daddy type.

Hunter stood up, wiped his hands on the back of his denim shorts. "Why, Angerman? Why're you so dead set on taking those two with you?"

Angerman stopped hammering. And then he said, in a strange, almost frightened voice, "The Grow Up." The voice was strange because it wasn't the anchorman voice or Angerman's regular voice but another voice altogether.

"The—Grow Up?" Hunter repeated, confused. "Y'mean that thing in Teacher's doorway?"

But Angerman wasn't answering any more questions. "Hand me one of those screwdrivers over there, wouldja?" he muttered in his regular voice. He curved his body away from Hunter and started hammering on the bolt again.

Mommy woke up before everyone else. The sky was still dark, and through the window next to her bed she could see a star, a single star, winking in the vast black sky.

It was the Big Day.

The girls were still sleeping, their bodies curved together like spoons. Baby was snoring, and Doll was murmuring something about toy trains. Mommy pushed herself up and over them, felt her bare feet touch the carpet, and padded into the hallway.

She listened. Nobody up yet. She began walking down the hall, not being able to see in the dark but knowing exactly what was in front of her, where she was going. She reached out her hand like a blind person: This part of the wall, that was where Baby and Doll had scribbled dolly pictures with their crayons. This crinkly paper, that was the poster of the Grown-up wearing white clothes and hitting a ball with a long smooth wooden stick. This cool edge of doorway, that was the boys' room. This knob, that was the linen closet.

She went downstairs. In the living room, Angerman was asleep in his usual chair, his head bobbing. Puppy and Kitty were curled up on the couch under a single afghan. Bad Guy was all the way across the room, tied up to the TV with the cable cord.

Their belongings—the family's belongings—were packed up and piled high by the front door, ready to go.

Outside, the birds had started to chirp. Mommy loved that sound, it was so familiar. She padded into the kitchen and began rummaging through the cupboards for breakfast. For the last time, the thought struck her, and she felt sadness grip her heart like a vise.

All the things had been packed up into backpacks and into one of the covered wagons. Baby and Doll got onto their matching pink bikes. Teddy Bear swung his leg over his red one. Teacher, Puppy, and Kitty—everyone was taking his place.

Mommy tried to make herself breathe normal breaths, willed her heart to stop racing.

"Time to go," Angerman announced. He was standing at the bottom of the driveway, cupping his hand over his eyes and staring up at the sun. It was already blazing hot.

Mommy hovered in the hallway, the last one out of the house. She gripped and ungripped her fists. She could feel the nausea rising in her stomach, the sour taste of bile in her throat. *Just calm down, just calm down, just calm down,* she told herself, closing her eyes.

A loud, bumpy, clanky noise. Mommy's eyes flew open. Hunter was backing Angerman's bike onto the front stoop, with the bike-wagon attachment swinging behind it. He then backed the whole thing into the hallway, parked it right smack in front of Mommy.

"Here," he said, opening up the bright red nylon flaps. "Just climb inside here, and I'll pull you out the door. So you won't have to—y'know."

Mommy smiled at him. "Okay. Thanks."

She glanced around one last time—the faded plaid couch, the speckled white kitchen counter, the toys they didn't have room for scattered all over the living room rug—and then climbed into the covered wagon. It creaked with the weight of her. A minute later, she felt Hunter pulling her out the door, over the stoop.

Bumpity-bump. Good-bye, house.

"Ya-ya-ya," she heard Action Figure crowing. "Goin to Washton!"

"Shhh, just go to sleep, Dolly, we'll be there soon," she heard Doll say.

The inside of the wagon had a new, fakey smell. Mommy felt warm, could already feel her skin beading with sweat. She opened the nylon flaps ever so slightly. The sandy driveway. The children all lined up on their bikes. The street. The sky.

And Angerman straddling his bike in front of them all, holding the picture frame to his face. "Now this live report," he said in his anchorman voice. "A group of children was seen leaving 24 Mango Street this morning on a fleet of bicycles. Sources indicated that they were heading north, toward Washington. We'll keep you posted as events unfold!"

Mommy closed the flap and slumped back in her seat and tried very hard not to scream.

Chapter Eleven

"Good-bye driveway!"

"Good-bye flower!"

"Good-bye pelican sitting on the house!"

Baby and Doll giggled. It was all a game to them, pedaling their little pink bikes and waving farewell at each thing they passed. Angerman stood on the pedals to pull the wagon with Mommy in it up a slight rise in the road. It was going to be a long trip.

Long. Long. Long. Two hours and fifty-four minutes approximate flying time to Dallas, ladies and gentle gentle—Longer than you can cuss for, the state capital of Long Island Sound is—

Angerman jabbed his elbow back, cracking Bad Guy a good one in the ribs. That would shut him up for a while anyway.

"You're sure this road leads north, right?" he called over to Hunter.

Hunter was squinting ahead, trying to toss the hair out of his eyes without releasing the handlebars. "It comes to a crisscross in a little while where there's a school bus, and then we'll turn onto a big road with yellow lines in the middle."

"State road? County road? Interstate?"

"Dunno. Lookout, Teddy!"

Teacher let out a small cry as Teddy Bear's bike swerved close to hers. Ignoring the boy's pleading look,

Teacher quickened her pace, pulling ahead until she was leading the convoy. Angerman thought he heard Bad Guy whispering behind his back.

The motorcade here comes the motorcade stand back make room wheeeeeee! Hail to the Chief and our compliments to the chef—

"Shut up," Angerman muttered.

"What?" There was a *zzzzz* as Mommy unzipped the cover and peeked out. "Did you say something?"

Angerman didn't reply. He was concentrating on keeping Bad Guy from shooting his mouth off or tangling his plastic ankles in the spokes, and it took all the energy he had to spare from pumping the bike pedals. His head bowed, Angerman watched the road sliding by beneath the wheels. A branch appeared in the path: his bike tires rolled along the side of it, but the cart wheels caught with a bump that almost jerked him off his seat.

"Idiot!" He jabbed Bad Guy again with his elbow, hard enough to make himself wince.

Doll let out a screech, and her bike wobbled to a stop. "Look!" She grabbed her dolly out of the front basket and held it up so it could see, too.

Angerman raised his head, saw Teacher circling back at Doll's cry. The sun hit him smack in the face, reflecting off a large building with one wall made entirely of huge square panes of glass. Some were broken, but it was mostly intact and gave back a gleaming picture of the trees, the clouds, the blue sky, the abandoned cars. A giant mirror. At the very top, stretching into the sky, was a cross. An osprey sat on one arm, preening itself.

"Big house," Action Figure said.

"That's not a house," Teacher told him. She swung her leg over her bike and hopped off. "That's a church. I'm going inside, see if there's any—"

"NO!" Angerman felt his voice coming out too loud, tried to make it right. "No, don't go in."

"You been in there?" Hunter asked suspiciously. "Is something in there?"

Mommy unzipped the flaps again and held them around her face. "What's wrong? Why did we stop?"

Teacher flipped down the kickstand with her foot. "I'm going into this—"

"No!" Angerman's voice came out right this time, the voice that made people listen. The Persuader Voice. He glanced at Hunter. "I've never been in there—how could I? I never was in this jerkwater town before. I just don't think Teacher should go in there."

"Why do you want to, Teacher?" Mommy asked, already withdrawing by degrees into the safety of the tent. The sun shining through the nylon of the wagon attached to Hunter's bike showed the shadowy silhouettes of Puppy and Kitty.

"I thought I'd find some good paper in there," Teacher explained with obvious irritation. "Good words I could put in The Book."

The Good Word, the Good Book, listen to the Good Word, brothers and sisters, my dear DEAR friends, and let us bow our heads in the covenant of the ReDEEMer! Thousands of the faithful gathered today in the Church of the Most Holy Blood of the Lamb outside Fort Wayne, Indiana—

Angerman stopped, saw them looking at him That

Way. He had the picture frame clutched so hard in his hand, his hand raised to his face, that his knuckles were white around the scabs and scratches. He lowered it, put it back in the front basket of his bike.

"Sorry."

He saw Hunter and Teacher exchange a quick look. Teacher shrugged and walked back to her bike as though she didn't care. Baby and Doll were whispering together, picking some kind of seed pods off some weeds. Some of the weeds were still flowering, their pink heads nodding in a breeze.

Pink blossoms. Trees with pink blossoms. And bridges, and long black cars.

"I'm okay," Angerman said, putting his Real Normal smile on his face. "Come on. We've got a long way to go before we get to Washington, so let's try to not waste any time."

He hitched his orange backpack a bit higher on his shoulders, hating the weight of Bad Guy but not daring to let him loose. Keeping Bad Guy away from Puppy and Kitty was too important to take chances. That was why he had insisted Puppy and Kitty ride behind Hunter, where Bad Guy wouldn't be staring at them with his horrible flat eyes.

"Okay back there?" he asked Mommy.

Mommy's voice was muffled. "I'm fine."

"Okay, then, let's keep going."

A cloud passed over the sun, turning the glass wall of the church black. Three flashing green parakeets shot out of a hole in the building and darted into a thicket of vine-choked trees. Gone. Gone. Gone. There was no one and nothing to see the small parade of children leave

Lazarus behind. In a few minutes, when Angerman looked back over his shoulder again, the town had been swallowed up in the thick jungle as totally as the birds.

Their progress was slow. The little kids weren't used to riding their bikes such long distances—neither were Hunter or Teacher or Angerman, for that matter—and they kept asking for rests. On top of that, Action Figure kept bolting off on detours, forcing them to wait until he joined them again. Mommy sat in the wagon, her knees drawn up, trying to keep from flying into a thousand pieces. She made herself breathe shallow, even breaths. The air was stuffy, but she was afraid to open the zipper. Besides, every time she looked up through the filmy plastic window, there was Bad Guy staring at her from where he was strapped to Angerman's backpack. So she had to keep looking out the sides, her view restricted to the wheels, pedals, and legs of the other kids. Whenever Hunter rode close, she could see Puppy and Kitty crouched in the wagon behind his bike. Teacher had to be somewhere out in front, because Mommy couldn't get a glimpse of her. The voices of the girls drifted to her in pieces. When she craned her neck to see out the back, she saw a sign, LAZARUS 3 MILES, and her heart sank. It would take them forever to get to Washington, D.C. It would take years.

Doll's voice became more insistent. Mommy heard the steady whine grow louder and more teary. She unzipped her door a fraction, letting in a whiff of fresh air.

"What's wrong with Doll?" she asked, trying not to look at Bad Guy, his horrible smooth plastic skin.

Angerman didn't answer. Mommy cringed, wondering how much he must resent having to pull her behind him this way. He pedaled steadily, hardly ever coasting.

"Angerman, stop. What's wrong with the girls?"

His legs stopped, and he squeezed the brake handle so abruptly that the wagon swung out to the left. Mommy grabbed wildly at the sides, looking for something to hang on to. The bike rolled to a stop.

"She's hungry."

Angerman turned around on the seat and looked back at her, his expression unreadable. "Doll is hungry and so is Baby and so is Teddy. I am not hungry."

Mommy leaned out a little bit, looking around. They were on a street crowded with cars, cars backed up, three deep, coming from four directions and jamming an intersection. Doors were open, suitcases were scattered, their contents long since soaked and rotted by five years of weather. Some cars were sprouting rank shrubbery through their open windows.

"We should stop for lunch," Mommy said. "Maybe we can find a—"

"A nice restaurant?" Angerman asked.

Hunter and Teacher walked their bikes over for a conference, while the younger kids let their bikes fall and sat in the shade of a large truck. Being so dependent on Angerman, Mommy was helpless to argue with him. She reached through the opening and tapped Hunter's leg until he looked at her. She nodded at the other children panting in the shade by the truck's flat tires.

"Bones?" she whispered. "Can you go check?"

He nodded, tilting his bike onto its kickstand, then

strolling along the line of cars, ducking and peering inside and around the abandoned vehicles. An opossum, roused from its sleep, waddled off into the tall grass. In a few moments, Hunter came back, shaking his head.

"I don't know where they all went," he said.

Teacher was cradling The Book inside its pillowcase, holding it like a baby. "They must've all left their cars and walked away."

"Where—to Lazarus?" Angerman asked. He hooted. "Did you guys notice a lot of dead strangers when it all happened?"

Mommy hugged herself, gripping her elbows. "We don't remember."

"I know, I know," Angerman replied. He pulled up his T-shirt hem and wiped his face with it. "Nobody remembers nothing. Do you even know if you were from Lazarus?"

Teacher had a glazed look in her eyes and didn't answer. Hunter squeezed the brake handle on his bike and released, squeezed and released. "I think I was. And Action."

"I can just picture it," Angerman continued in a cheery voice. "All these people get out of their cars, already dying, and start staggering their way to Lazarus. Must have been a really interesting parade, huh?"

"Cut it out," Hunter said.

But Angerman wouldn't shut up. He unbuckled his backpack as he spoke, almost without seeming to know he was doing it. "Really nice picture to have in your head, isn't it? They grab their stuff, they're looking for water, looking for a doctor, maybe. I bet they're trying to carry their kids, kids are following, they don't know what's wrong, why all the adults are sick. Daddy! Mommy!"

Mommy, Teacher, and Hunter gaped at him in horror. Angerman had lowered Bad Guy to the ground and was slowly, methodically, scraping the mannequin's plastic face on the broken pavement of the road, gouging big furrows into the nose and cheeks and tearing away the shreds of tape.

"And so all along the way into Lazarus, people are dropping dead, just like that, and the kids are all left alone, wandering around, and animals start eating the dead bodies and most of the kids end up dead, too, because they're too little, or they get hurt and no one can help them."

Hunter stepped forward and put his hand on Angerman's shoulder. "Hey. Hey."

"What?" Angerman looked up. He looked insane.

Mommy covered her face with her hands. What were they doing? This trip was hopeless. They were following a lunatic off the edge of the world.

"Mommy?" Teddy Bear ran over and patted the side of the wagon. "Mommy, can't we have something to eat?" Mommy saw him glance down at Bad Guy's ravaged face, up at Angerman, and then at Teacher.

"You can have some water," Teacher said.

"Oh, come on—we can stop for a while and eat something. There's army guy ration protein bars I found at the army navy store," Hunter said, cajoling. "We'll find another supermarket before long and we'll have plenty of food. We don't have to be so cheap anymore."

"And we—you guys—need your strength," Mommy said. She blushed, knowing she was a burden. "Let's all take a break. But how about over in the shade?"

Angerman didn't answer, but he didn't object, either. He picked up Bad Guy and in a flash, unzipped Mommy's wagon all the way, thrusting Bad Guy in with her. She had to stifle a scream. "Just let him ride with you for a second," he said, straddling the bike again.

Shuddering, Mommy pushed Bad Guy over against the side with the back of one hand, and poked him again so that he wouldn't be looking at her. His legs stuck out through the zippered opening. Angerman began riding toward the shadow of the big tractor trailer, and Mommy was torn between the need to get away from the mannequin and the fear of leaving her shelter.

Then, as Angerman squeezed the bike between two cars, Mommy felt a slap in her heart. "Stop!" she croaked. "Stop the bike!"

Angerman looked back at her, braking. "What is it? Did he say something?"

Mommy sat staring at a red minivan just ahead of them. The rear door was plastered with bumper stickers—WBBF PUBLIC RADIO. I BRAKE FOR MANATEES. MY CHILD WAS STUDENT OF THE MONTH AT MANGROVE ELEMENTARY. UNIVERSITY OF MIAMI. IF YOU CAN READ THIS YOU DON'T NEED A LITERACY TUTOR. Mommy could feel that screaming spirit dashing through her, dashing. Her hands shook as she parted the flaps of the wagon. Waves of heat streamed over her skin like sticky hands.

"Are you getting out?" Angerman asked, obviously surprised.

The screaming spirit was in her throat. Mommy made it stay down, although it was such an effort that every muscle in her body jumped and quivered with the strain. She heard a noise, and realized it was her breath, harsh and quick. She gripped the bumper of the minivan and pulled herself upright, stepping out over Bad Guy's legs. Then she dragged herself along the side of the car, pressing her back against it as though she traversed a narrow ledge over a chasm. She panted, squeezing her eyes shut, and then turned to look into the van.

A car seat. A set of colorful plastic toy keys on a big plastic ring. An empty potato chip bag, snack size. And on the floor of the backseat, a book. Mommy fumbled with the door handle, jabbing with her thumb on the knob as she pulled, leaning all her weight to it. The door stuck, then slid open. A wave of damp heat poured out of the car, but Mommy ignored it. She reached for the book.

It was paperback called *Ring of Bright Water*. She saw her hands open the cover of the book, heard an unsteady thudding in her ears. On the inside cover, written in ink, was a name: Annie Ginkel, in big, looping letters, with circles to dot the *I*s.

Mommy could feel the others—Teacher, Hunter, and Angerman—standing behind her. Angerman stepped closer and read over her shoulder. She could feel his breath on her cheek.

Finally, he spoke, his voice very gentle. "Is this your book? Was this your family's car?"

Mommy began to weep, in huge, wrenching cries that seemed to split her open like an axe. "I don't know," she sobbed. "I don't remember."

And her heart was breaking because really, really, she wasn't sure.

Chapter Twelve

Hunter moved through the dark lobby of the Rondayvoo Motel. It wasn't morning yet, and so it was hard to see. He swept his flashlight beam around the perimeter, tried to remember the terrain from when they'd checked in last night. The coffee machine. The table with the vase of plastic flowers. The handwritten sign that said *No Out-of-State-Checks Will Be Honered.* The venetian blind that hung crookedly in the window, its slats skewed this way and that like bones.

The place was silent. No one else up yet, just him. Even Action Figure was still asleep, not off on some maneuver as usual. The long, hot bike ride had wiped everyone out.

Just before sunset, they had found the Rondayvoo on a wide stretch of road full of motels and other places. McDonald's. Burger King. The Home Depot. Wal-Mart. Probably good hunting in those spots, but they didn't have the time—or the space in their cargo wagon, either. Right now, Hunter had to focus on a few essentials.

The most important of which was water. Bike riding in the hot sun made them so thirsty they drank more than they could carry.

From upstairs, he heard the soft creak of a footstep. Someone up. They had taken over the entire second floor. A whole row of rooms overlooking the parking lot with its half dozen dead cars, a dirty white yacht blown off its trailer, and a sign that would have flashed RONDAYVOO MOTEL VACANCY FREE CABLE HOT TUBS had there been electricity. Of course, Hunter had come in first, to sweep for bones. He had found a bunch of them, managed to shove them into a coat closet before the little ones had burst in demanding to see their "new house."

Crrrack. Something under his foot. He bent down and swung the flashlight around. Some dead palmetto bugs, an empty bottle of Richard's Wild Irish Rose. Near his boot, broken in half, a woman's red plastic hairbrush snarled with blond hairs. There was also a pair of glasses. He snapped them open and put them on, tipping his head up to see how his vision was. Everything was double. He ripped them off his face and tossed them away.

Hunter rose and kept moving. Maybe he'd check the halls for vending machines. Those could be useful if they still had stuff in them, and he could bust the glass panels with a hammer. Mostly those machines were full of Bonuses, which Mommy wouldn't let the little ones have too often due to Cavities. There were no dentists around anymore, so Cavities could mean Infections. And even worse. There might be some small bottles of water, though.

Why was there no water anywhere? Hunter wondered. Yesterday they had stopped three, four times at various grocery stores, looking for those big plastic jugs of it. But the shelves had been wiped clean of them. He supposed that was what people had gone for first, when Fire-us hit. Everyone panicking. State of Emergency. Adults burning up.

Riding their bikes in the hot sun yesterday, the

family had gone through the contents of their water bottles in no time. And collecting rainwater wasn't an option any more. *What now? What next?* It was Hunter's job to hunt—he had to figure this out before it became a serious problem.

A refrigerator.

Hunter did a double take, swung his flashlight around. He hadn't noticed it last night, tucked into an alcove behind the front desk. He walked over to it, stepping around a couple of overturned chairs, a dead lizard.

He tugged at the refrigerator door. It was stuck. He tugged harder. There was a soft sucking sound of a vacuum breaking, and the door swung open on rusty hinges.

Hunter cursed, staggered back. The smell—the *smell*—was unbearable. There was something on the top shelf, what might once have been a sandwich. The corpse of it was hidden in a bright orange and blue wrapper that said SAMI'S SUB SHOPPE. There were some bottles of beer, half a flask of gin. Brown shapeless lumps that might have been oranges. And mold everywhere.

On the bottom shelf were three plastic jugs of water. Bingo. Holding his breath in, Hunter lifted the jugs and kicked the door shut with one foot. There would be enough for teeth brushing and face washing this morning, and some left over to fill the water bottles for the next leg of their trip.

He headed up with the bottles, feeling almost lighthearted: a successful hunt. Morning light was beginning to seep through the grimy windows.

Upstairs, everyone was up, congregated in the room

Mommy shared with the girls. Doll and Baby were bouncing up and down on one of the beds, chanting a song about Cereos and "chocklit pudding." Action Figure was trying to rip out a thick metal chain that fastened the useless TV set to the floor. Teddy Bear was hobbling around, holding his crotch and moaning, "Gotta pee, I gotta pee." Puppy and Kitty were huddled in a corner under a rumpled white sheet, sniveling. Mommy was hovering over them, wiping their noses and murmuring, "Shhh, just a bad dream." Angerman was standing at the window, staring out at the wrecked boat.

"Where's Teacher?" Hunter said, setting the jugs of water on the dresser. He rubbed his forearm muscles. Everything ached.

Teddy Bear stopped his hobbling for a second and stared up at Hunter. "She said she had to c'lect Information. Hunter, my legs hurt. From all that bikin'."

"Mine too," Baby chimed in.

"Mine three," Doll added. "Dolly wants to know if we can just stay in our new house today and rest."

Angerman whirled around. "No!"

Action Figure glanced up from his tug-of-war games with the chain. "Gotta be men. Gotta be tough!" he barked at Teddy Bear and the girls.

"But my *legs* hurt," Teddy Bear said, sniffling. "Can't bike no more."

Action Figure marched over to him. "Gotta be tough," he repeated. "Gotta get to Washton today!" He gave Teddy Bear a little shove.

"Action!" Mommy snapped.

Teddy Bear began to wail. A stain spread across the front of his pajama bottoms. Baby leaped off the bed and engulfed Teddy Bear in a big hug. "Shhh, just a bad dream," she cooed.

Hunter rushed over to Action Figure, grabbed him by the arm. "You. Come with me. Now!"

Action Figure struggled to free himself. "Lemme go!"

Hunter tightened his grip. When did his brother get so strong? "You cannot be mean to the other kids. Understand? You cannot order the other kids around, or push them, either."

Action Figure gave Hunter a look of pure fury. "Kin do whatever I wanna," he hissed. And then he wrenched his arm away from Hunter and ran, flew out of the room.

Hunter started to follow his brother, then stopped. It was useless, Action Figure had grown wild as a panther—there was no reaching him anymore. Hunter went back to the dresser, where he had left the three jugs of water. But the happiness from his good hunt was gone, and he felt nothing, nothing as he lifted one of the jugs and called out to the little ones, "C'mon, wash faces, then I'll round us up some breakfast."

Teacher wandered over to the front desk and sat down on the squeaky swivel chair. So noisy up on the second floor, with the strays bawling and the others clamoring for food and whatnot. This would be a good, quiet place to work.

Action Figure raced by the desk and out the front door. Teacher barely glanced up.

She reached into her pillowcase and pulled out The Book. She blew on the desk, watched a cloud of dust rise up, then set the volume down ever so gently. Then she reached back into the pillowcase and pulled out her supplies: a pencil, a bottle of glue, a pair of rusty but perfectly good scissors.

She was tired, tired. Up all night, recording dreams. She had gone from room to room—the rooms had been identical except for the numbers on the doors—and listened to the children babbling and crying and moaning in their sleep. Leaving Lazarus had made everyone dream a lot. The tips of her fingers were sore and wrinkly like prunes from all the writing.

Now it was time to examine what she had written. She let her pruney fingertips hover over The Book and closed her eyes. Let her fingertips trail across the smooth, hard cover, drop down to the rough, crinkly edge of the pages.

Open The Book. Open her eyes.

PUPPY SAYS INGRID WANTS MORE
LEMONADE.

The words leaped out at her like sparks. She felt dizzy and had to cradle her head with her hands to still the swirling and swaying. The words were in her handwriting. But she didn't remember writing them.

And what did these words mean? she wondered. Did Puppy actually say them, or had she just imagined it? After all, Puppy didn't talk words. He just barked and whined like a runt dog, like he had from the very beginning.

Curiosity gnawed at her. She got up from the desk, put The Book and her supplies back in the pillowcase, and started upstairs. She had to ask Puppy about the words right away.

But before she got to the stairs, something caught

her eye. A rack of brochures. Faded photos of palm trees, alligators, Grown-ups basking by a glittering blue pool. *Your Guide to Northwest Florida. Welcome to the Land of Nonstop Sun and Fun!*

Teacher grabbed one of the brochures and opened it. Information. *New* Information. She felt greedy, excited, palms sweaty, as if it were Christmas morning.

There was a cartoonish map inside of the roads in the area. *Good.* The other brochures had the same. Teacher doubled back to the desk and glued the brochures into The Book before heading upstairs again.

She found Puppy in Mommy's room, huddled under a sheet with Kitty. Angerman was standing by the window, just a few feet away from them. The others were sitting cross-legged on the two double beds while Mommy and Hunter fed them dried beef sticks.

Teacher crossed the room and knelt down by Puppy. "Who's Ingrid?"

Puppy stared up at her with his big brown eyes and said nothing.

Teacher turned to Kitty. "Are *you* Ingrid? Is that your name?"

Kitty stared up at her. She didn't say a word, either, just huddled closer to Puppy.

"I NEED TO KNOW—WHO IS INGRID?" Teacher demanded.

Angerman turned from the window. "Stop it, just stop it," he ordered her.

Teacher opened her mouth, then clamped it shut. Puppy and Kitty scrambled to their feet and ran over to Angerman, barking and meowing. They clung to his legs while he stroked their heads, murmuring soothing little words that meant nothing at all. Were useless.

"My legs hurt!"

"My arms hurt!"

"I'm thirsty—can't we stop? Pleeeaze?"

Listening to Baby's, Doll's, and Teddy Bear's complaints made Angerman pedal even harder. He swiped the back of his hand across his brow, felt sweat pouring down the back of his neck and shoulders. The sun was terrible, grueling. And as far as he could tell, it wasn't even noon yet.

They were going down something called Route 16. Past office parks. Past a billboard that said, MANATEE MINIPUTT, ½ MILE! Past a bunch of low flat buildings with fleets of trucks out front. There was a big bronze sign that said BAILEY INDUSTRIAL PARK. Vines tangling, curling over the edges of it, and a couple of seagulls sitting on top, shrieking and jabbing at each other with their hooked beaks.

Won't you come home Bill Bailey won't you come home—home! Home, house, white. Whiten your teeth with Dentamint. Wheeee! Looky out for that big bump in the road, Anger-whatever it is you're calling yourself these days, ya never know what can happen if you're not careful!

Angerman put on the brakes. Behind him, he could feel Bad Guy sliding down his back, getting tangled up in the spokes. Angerman cursed. He would have to hitch him up on his back better, with more rope.

Still, at least that shut him up for the moment,

Angerman thought.

Teacher stopped her bike next to his. The other children stopped behind her and waited while Angerman adjusted his load.

"That's the third time this morning," Teacher said. "Can't you just ditch that stupid thing? Why do you have to bring it, anyway?"

Awww, don't let her talk about me like that!

"Quiet," Angerman hissed.

Teacher raised her eyebrows. "What? Did you say something?"

Angerman shook his head. "No, nothing. That is, I said—I *have* to bring him."

"But why?" Teacher persisted. The others were silent.

"Never mind," Angerman muttered. Didn't she get it? End of topic. Not open to discussion.

And for the ambassador of Austria, we will be serving roasted quail with fresh figs and a light Gorgonzola sauce—

Angerman whirled around, grabbed Bad Guy by the neck, and squeezed. Hard. He could almost imagine the horrible flat eyes bugging out, the beige lips turning purply-blue. Good, let him gasp for breath—at least he won't be able to talk anymore. He needed another gag of some kind, more tape or something.

Mommy unzipped the flaps of the wagon and poked her head out. "Um, what's going on?"

"Nothing, nothing," Angerman said. He let go of Bad Guy's neck and smiled through clenched teeth.

Everything under control, move along, folks, go

about your business.

Mommy frowned at him and zipped the flaps back up. Angerman strapped Bad Guy onto his backpack, extratight this time.

A few minutes later, he started pedaling again, and the others followed.

The road curved ahead. As they turned, they came upon a strange sight: a meadow overgrown with tall grass. Statues everywhere—a windmill, a lighthouse, a giant bear, a miniature castle. Out past the fence that surrounded it was a meadow with grazing cattle and white egrets stalking through the grass.

The sign out front read MANATEE MINIPUTT.

Baby was the first to slam on her brakes. "MiniPutt!" she squealed. "Isn't that a game, Teacher? Didn't you learn us that in School?"

Doll put on her brakes, too. "Yes, issa a game, can we please play, can we please?"

Teddy Bear and Action Figure joined in the chorus. "Let's play, let's play, let's play!"

Angerman felt rage swell up inside him. The group was making such slow progress as it was. How could they stop and do this useless thing, waste even more time?

He put his brakes on and turned to the little ones. "No, no way! We have to make as much distance as we can while it's light out."

Teacher pulled up beside him and put her hand on his arm. "Come on—give 'em a break. They need to do something fun."

Angerman was about to protest. But then he saw the faces of the little ones watching him, waiting. "Oh, all right," he said with a sigh. "Just for a few minutes, though."

The children shrieked and let their bikes fall to the ground with a loud crash and tumble of metal. They ran toward the giant bear, the windmill, the castle. Even Puppy and Kitty got out of their wagon and ran after the others.

Angerman watched them, willing Bad Guy to be silent. And he was.

Chapter Thirteen

Laughing, shouting, the little ones veered toward the small building at the entrance. It was a sort of shed with a counter where people were supposed to pay and get their golf clubs. Angerman wheeled his bike into its shade. The screams and shrieks of the children rebounded from the ceiling as they pawed through the rusty pile of putters and drivers. Mommy took a deep breath, shut her eyes, and lunged out of the wagon, rocketing herself toward the safety of the shed. She pulled herself around behind the counter and sat on the stool. Teddy Bear squeezed in front of her legs as he hunted under the counter for balls.

"We can pretend I work here," Mommy said in a strained effort at sounding comfortable and cheery. She yanked at a drawer that was swollen with moisture. It finally screeched open, showing a mildewy stack of par sheets and stubby pencils. Her hands trembled as she took the scorecards out.

"Whassat thing?" Action Figure demanded, pointing at a red-and-white-striped windmill in the fourth hole. The blades of the windmill were broken, and the paint was faded. A long withered palm frond rested against the side, making an awning for the little hole the ball was supposed to go into.

Teacher glanced at where he pointed. "In olden days those arms would turn around and around in the wind and move machinery inside."

Hunter stared. "How do you remember that?"

"Just do."

Mommy kept her head down, separating the damp scorecards and handing one to each of the kids, who were hopping with impatience, not even sure what to do with each piece of equipment but determined to play putt-putt the Right Way. When they each had a ball and a club and a scorecard, they scattered like sparrows, bossing each other around and arguing over where to start. Hunter and Teacher followed more slowly, to clear the dried-out palm fronds that littered the course. With a quick look through the hair that fell down over her face, Mommy checked that they were all happy and busy, and tried not to shiver. The sky was so big. The metal feet of her stool screeched across the cement as she scooted back a bit farther inside the shed. Out past the putt-putt course, on the broad field of wet grass, the egrets stalked for bugs or piggybacked on the cattle's bony spines.

Angerman dragged another stool over to the counter and sat beside Mommy. He put a bottle of soda in front of her, grinning triumphantly.

"Look what I found," he said as he opened one for himself. He swigged it thirstily and then let out a groan of contentment. "This stuff used to be fizzy. 'Member the bubbles? I wonder where they went?"

Mommy traced the lettering on her bottle with one finger. "Same place everything else normal went." She tried to say what was on her mind and frowned, searching for words. "Look, I feel so dumb having to get pulled—making you have to pull me. I should be able to—"

"Forget it." Angerman scratched his scalp, and examined his fingernails with interest. Then he looked at her, his eyes sharp. "Do you ever wonder if we're all crazy?"

Mommy couldn't answer. A hot flush washed up her throat.

"I mean, do you ever wonder if any of this really happened?" he went on, hitching his stool closer to her and leaning in, earnest and fiery. "This is all crazy stuff—maybe we're all crazy and we're dreaming this."

A high, excited laugh from one of the children broke into Mommy's thoughts. She looked out to where Baby and Doll were jostling each other to hit their balls through a covered bridge. Action Figure and Teddy Bear were competing against each other near a dried-up fountain, and Teddy Bear was laughing almost hysterically, swinging and missing, swinging and missing, laughing himself silly. Puppy and Kitty obviously didn't understand what they were supposed to do; they were smacking happily with their clubs on the top of a cement snowman. Mommy shook her head, feeling that painful twist of the heart the little ones produced.

"I wish we were dreaming," she said. "But I don't think we are."

Hunter and Teacher joined them in the shed, reaching for the soda bottles Angerman had lined up on the counter.

"Good hunt," Hunter said with a smile, and raised his bottle in a salute to Angerman.

Teacher twisted the cap off her bottle, and then swigged a short swallow while she unwrapped The Book from its pillowcase. Mommy stilled herself at the sight of The Book, awed by that church feeling it gave her, and knew Hunter felt it, too. But Angerman reached for it casually, sliding it closer toward him to see. Teacher tensed, and a frown pulled her eyebrows together. Her hand tightened around her soda.

Clearing his throat, Hunter told Angerman, "Hey, uh, you're not supposed to touch that."

"Huh?" Angerman looked up, hand poised over the cover he was about to open. "Oh. Sorry," he said, and pulled away.

Teacher gave him a tight, prim smile. "It's okay, I guess. It's just that I'm the one that usually—"

"No, forget it, I understand," Angerman cut in. He hopped down from his stool and ushered Teacher into his place beside Mommy.

A little sigh of relief passed Teacher's lips. She hiked herself up onto the stool and opened The Book while Mommy, Hunter, and Angerman looked over her bony shoulders.

"Here's where I found the maps," Teacher began, opening the thick scrapbook with her thumb.

"You mean where you put the maps," Angerman corrected her.

Teacher gave him a blank look. "No, this is the page where I found the maps," she insisted.

Mommy felt herself nodding. That's how it would be, she figured. The Book had everything in it already, but Teacher had to study it to discover the Information they needed. Angerman looked puzzled, but he just shrugged while Teacher opened to the right page.

"Did you see me, Mommy?" Teddy Bear called from

afar. "Did you see me get it in the hole?"

"Sure did!" Mommy replied and looked up with a swift smile. "Great shot!"

"I'm winning!" he added. "Action is winning, too! So's Baby and so's Doll!"

Mommy waved. "I'm so proud of you!"

When she turned her attention back to the others, they all had their fingers on the cartoonish maps, pointing to one blue line or red line or another. Hunter kept jabbing the page.

"Look, if we stick to the small roads that go through towns, we'll find all kinds of stuff we can use. Bottled water. Tons of food. Clothes. Anything."

"But it would be a lot slower," Angerman pointed out. "I say we stick to the interstate, it's pretty much straight and it'd be faster. See how squiggly the local roads are? We'd be going twice as far."

Hunter began kicking the underside of the counter. It resounded with a hollow wooden thump at each kick. "But there isn't anything to hunt if we stick to that road."

"We can do both," Teacher said. "Stay on the small roads until the next real town and get supplies, and then hit the fast road."

The two boys looked at her in blank surprise. Mommy laughed at the expressions on their faces. "Gee, why didn't you think of that?" she teased them.

Teacher held out her hand and began ticking items off on her fingers. "We need more bottled water, definitely powdered milk or that kind of canned milk Hunter used to find—"

"Good for strong bones and teeth," Mommy recited

from memory from her *Family Health Guide.*

"Right." Teacher nodded. "Vitamins, good shoes, hats—"

"Hats?" Hunter broke in.

"The kids need hats—they're complaining about the sun," Teacher explained.

A flash of anger and embarrassment caught Mommy by surprise. She hadn't known the children were complaining about the sun in their eyes. She'd been stuck inside her little cocoon, cut off from everyone. As Teacher continued listing the things they needed, especially the things they needed for the little ones, sadness settled onto Mommy's shoulders and pushed them down. She was the one who was supposed to be taking care of the little ones. That was what she was best at. But here, out in the open, she didn't seem to be good for much at all. While the others planned, she slid off her stool and moved toward the back of the shed, into the tiny office with its desk and dead computer and telephone. From there, the sky was reduced to a thin strip between the shed roof and the counter, and even that was interrupted by Teacher, Hunter, and Angerman, thrown into silhouette by the bright light beyond them.

If she had nothing to give to her family, she was useless to them, and then why should they bother to drag her along with them? It would probably take months to find President—no, years, maybe—if he was even alive. How could she make them drag along a dead weight? And even if they did all stay together, how long could they really expect to be okay? At least at home they knew where they were and how to manage, but now that they had left all those familiar things behind, they had no idea what might lie in the road. If they did go on for years, getting older, did that mean that she and Teacher and Hunter and Angerman would get sick like all the other Grown-ups had? Would they die and leave their little children all alone—alone again?

Mommy sat in the desk chair, surrounded by the useless electronic machines from the Before Time. From her back pocket she pulled the book *Ring of Bright Water* that she had found in the red minivan.

She put it on the desk and pulled her hands away, unwilling to touch it even though she'd been carrying it all along. It sat there, closed, the illustration on the cover faded from the sun. As if she could see through the cover, Mommy saw the name inscribed inside it: Annie Ginkel, written in loopy script.

If she was Annie Ginkel, then the red minivan was her family's car. Some Grown-up had been driving it. And some baby had been in the safety seat. Hot tears welled up in Mommy's eyes and spilled over, and she brushed them away with a hand that felt as heavy as a stone.

It was better to believe she wasn't really a girl named Annie Ginkel. It was better to think of herself as Mommy, who had a family, with girls and boys who loved her and who were outside playing right now in the sunshine, giggling and making up silly rules for a game they didn't understand. That was what children were supposed to do. They were supposed to show each other things they'd found—shells and pinecones and things that looked like other things, like a pink rock that looked like a rabbit's head or a leaf in the shape of a Christmas tree.

Mommy looked up, swiping tears away, as Angerman came into the office. He opened a few drawers, rummaging around, pocketing things that struck him as useful—twine, a plastic bottle with six aspirins rattling in it, a screwdriver, a book of matches. Mommy watched him at his purposeful scavenging; he hardly even seemed to notice her sitting there in tears. What did he care? He was on a mission, and it didn't really matter to him anyway if they were coming with him or not. But here they were, wandering off into the wilderness with him, and anything terrible could happen tomorrow. Mommy felt herself getting stiffer and angrier as he made his way toward her. She thought that if he came any closer to her she would scream.

Angerman walked behind her chair, humming as he picked up and examined a battery-powered, handheld fan. He clicked the switch, but nothing happened. "Dead."

Coming from Angerman's mouth, that word pierced Mommy like a blade. She sprang out of her chair, shoving him backward. "Why did you have to come to us?" she cried.

Angerman looked startled, but he made no move to get out of her way. Mommy took a step toward him with her hand raised, and he still didn't get out of her way. "You've ruined everything," she said, dropping back into the chair and sobbing. "You've ruined everything."

Gently, Angerman put one hand on her shoulder and then pulled her close to let her weep against him. Mommy grabbed the fabric of his shirt in her fists, feeling her shoulders jerk with the violence of her sorrow. "I could kill you," she gasped.

"I know," Angerman said. "But listen, you have to remember something really important."

He paused. Mommy knew he wanted her to look at him. Catching her breath, she sat up and stared at him through burning eyes.

Angerman looked as sorrowful as she felt. "Just remember, it wasn't me who did all this."

She looked away, her gaze roaming over the lifeless computer, the telephone that would never ring, the minifridge that was good for nothing. "I know," she whispered. "But I want to blame somebody."

"Me, too."

Outside, the children had finished their golf and were clamoring for water and snacks. Mommy rubbed her face with both hands. "I guess we should get going again," she sighed.

"Yeah," Angerman said in a quiet voice. "Let's go."

Chapter Fourteen

They were coming into new terrain now, not fast-food restaurants and office buildings anymore but woods, a big lake, little cottages. The cottages had names like Sea Breeze and Hal's Hacienda and E-Z Livin'. As Hunter pedaled by them he tried to size them up for camping purposes. They seemed way too small, which meant they would have to take over several of them, like a compound. And they were far apart, which would make things tough panther-wise. Maybe best to keep looking, he thought.

Still, the sun was starting to fade, and the little ones were complaining about being tired, hungry, thirsty. Hunter's own stomach was grumbling. It would be nice to stop somewhere, set up camp, and dig into the provisions he'd hunted at Publix this afternoon. Canned tuna, peanut butter—really prime stuff.

Just then, he noticed two abandoned bikes in the road: a big one and a little kid one. A dead rat snake was coiled around the back spokes of the big one. Hunter's first thought was, *Too beat up and rusty to trade in for.* And then, *Wonder what happened to the owners?*

It occurred to Hunter then, not for the first time, how weird this all was. Going through new towns after being stuck in Lazarus for five years. So many exciting new things to see, new terrain. And yet all of it crazy and upside down, because there were no people anywhere, not even children.

Of course, it had been that way in Lazarus. And the rest of it, too—the dead cars covered with wet leaves and bird droppings, the broken glass, the bones. Nothing working because of the electricity, everything rotting and overgrown, plants growing rampant over everything. But somehow, Hunter had never imagined that the rest of Florida would be the same vast wasteland as Lazarus.

He glanced over at Angerman, who was pedaling beside him with the mannequin strapped to his back. Staring at the road, muttering to himself. Was it insane for the family to be following this guy to Washington? They hadn't found any people so far. How could they hope to find anyone in Washington, much less President?

Action Figure's voice cut into his thoughts. "Whassat over there? Big nice house."

Hunter looked up. Action Figure was pointing at a building in the distance.

"Looks like a Swiss chalet," Hunter said.

Action Figure frowned. "Huh?"

Hunter found himself grinning, almost laughing. *Where did that come from, "Swiss chalet"?* Such silly-sounding words. He had no idea what they meant or how he knew them.

"Let's check it out," Hunter told his brother.

Standing up on their bikes, Hunter and Action Figure took the lead while the rest of the family fell back. The road curved, following the edge of the lake. They passed privet bushes, acacia, and strangler figs, passed under silvery-green wisps of Spanish moss that curled down from the tops of the trees. The air smelled wonderful, like a real camping-in-the-woods smell.

They soon neared the building. It was big and brown

with a goofy-looking sloped roof, white windowboxes overflowing with weeds. There were a dozen cars in the parking lot with a giant oak tree toppled over them, nearly burying them in dead branches and green vines. Two jacaranda trees framed the doorway, their branches heavy with purple blossoms.

The sign out front said ALPENHAUS A FAMILY RESTAURANT.

Teacher pulled up next to Hunter. "We're meant to stay here," she whispered. "It's for families."

Hunter parked his bike next to a gray station wagon. "Let me just, um, check it out first. Can you keep everyone outside?"

Teacher nodded. "Of course."

Action Figure let his bike tumble to the ground next to Hunter's. "Lemme come!"

"No!" Hunter said. Then, seeing the hurt, angry look on his brother's face, added, "Give me five minutes, Action. Then I'll put you in charge of setting up the camping equipment. 'Kay?"

Action Figure pouted. "'Kay."

Hunter's foot went through the wooden step as he reached for the door. A mass of white, pulpy termites milled out of the rotting wood. Hunter shook them off his sneaker, and shouldered the door open. He didn't have much time before Action Figure would disobey his orders and follow him anyway. Not to mention the other little ones, who would be eager to explore.

Hunter paused at the wood-paneled bar and squinted, tried to get his bearings. There were lots of tables and chairs, some of them knocked over. Red-and-white tablecloths and napkins. Salt and pepper shakers, menus, little gold lamps with candles in them. A lot of bones.

Hunter cursed, then got busy. Arm, leg, skull, another arm. A whole intact skeleton draped across a red booth held together by the rotting shirt and pants. He started collecting them and piling them under one of the tables so that the tablecloth hid them from view. It was the fastest way.

Before he was done with his mission—Angerman referred to it as his "advance-team work," whatever that meant—he heard the door burst open behind him. He kicked one last bone under the table and turned around. Action Figure came running up to him, waving his bow and arrows in the air. "Lemme help!"

Hunter plastered a big, cheerful smile on his face. "Come on. You can help me carry the camping equipment inside—the tents and stuff. And then we'll set it up."

Action Figure's eyes darted away. A large green lizard was scurrying across the floor. The boy hoisted his bow to his shoulder and aimed one of his arrows.

"Come on—no time for hunting," Hunter said, grabbing his brother's arm. "We have to pitch camp before it gets dark. You can hunt tomorrow."

"Gonna kilt me some lizards and mebbe some birds," Action Figure said, smacking his lips.

On their way out, Hunter noticed something on one of the tables. A pair of glasses with dark lenses, totally intact. He flipped them open and put them on, hoping these would be good. Dark. Dark but clear. With a flood of happiness, Hunter took off the glasses and slipped them in his pocket. They would be perfect in the daytime.

Out in the parking lot, the other little ones were squatting on the curb, swatting each other with their new hats from Publix. Teacher was telling them a story from The Book. Mommy was listening to the story, too, and trying to get them to stop taunting each other. Hunter could just make out a sliver of her thin, pale face through the flaps of her wagon.

Angerman was still on his bike, rocking this way and that, muttering to himself. He seemed all worked up about something today.

"'I-95 comes in from the north and joins I-10 just south of downtown,'" Teacher read in a quiet voice. "'There are lovely shrubs and a view of the Saint Johns River. Blue Plate Specials every Tuesday night. Close to major attractions.' So says The Book."

Hunter cleared his throat. Teacher glanced up at him and closed The Book. "Ready?"

Hunter nodded. "Ready."

The children jumped up from the curb and swarmed into the Alpenhaus like ants. "They have choklit at this restyraunt!" Doll told her dolly.

"And manilla ice cream, too!" Baby added.

Angerman seemed to come out of his weird trance and jerked Mommy's covered wagon up and over the curb. "Hey! Watch it!" Mommy cried out. Hunter watched the wagon lean to the left, then disappear through the door.

Action Figure was tugging on Hunter's T-shirt. "C'mon, c'mon!"

Hunter grinned down at his brother. "Whatdyya think—we gotta get the mattress pads and the sleeping bags first. No need to get the candles and lamps, 'cause there's candles already in there. But matches, lots of matches. And the water bottles and the food rations."

"Ya-ya-ya," Action said, rushing over to the supply wagon.

As the two of them combed through their gear, Hunter felt that rush of happiness again. The sun was setting, and the sky was aflame with pinks, purples, reds. It was so beautiful here, with the lake and the trees and all. And here they were, he and Action Figure, working on a project together like in the old days. Just the guys, just a couple of men.

Hunter touched the dark glasses in his pocket. Things were definitely starting to look up.

Teacher sat at one of the tables alone, poring over The Book. The flame of the restaurant candle hissed at the air, made strange shadows on the crackly ancient paper. She bent her head way down and turned the page. She wasn't sure what she was looking for. Something, something was bothering her, though.

At the next couple of tables, Mommy, Hunter, Angerman, and the little ones were having canned tuna by candlelight. There was a huge picture window overlooking the lake, which was all shimmery with the colors of the sunset. A lake of fire. Teacher had to admit, it was pretty here. And the little ones were giggling, feeding each other peanut butter off fingers, having a grand old time. Even Puppy and Kitty.

Baby thumped her water bottle on the table. "More water, more water!" she demanded.

Mommy reached over and passed a canteen to her.

"Here you go, honey."

"Dolly and I want water, too," Doll piped up.

"Me, too," Teddy Bear mumbled, his mouth full of peanut butter.

"Baby, you give that canteen to the others when you're done," Mommy instructed. "Teacher, are you working on our route for tomorrow?"

Teacher was about to reply when Baby turned the canteen upside down and shook it. A couple of drops dribbled onto the table. "All gone!"

Doll began to wail. "What about Dolly and me?"

Mommy sighed. "Hunter? Where's the rest of the water?"

Hunter squirmed in his chair. "Where's the—well, that was it. That was all we had."

"What!" Mommy gasped.

Teacher felt anger swell up in her. Anger and panic. "Weren't you keeping track?" she asked Hunter.

"It's my job to hunt. It's not my job to ration every last bit of food and water we have!" Hunter retorted. "Don't forget, I hunted us some water at the motel this morning, and then a couple of quarts of it at Publix. But I guess we used all that up."

Teacher sucked in a deep breath. "We need to be clearer about who's in charge of what!" she said to no one in particular. "There are things at stake. This isn't a vacation, y'know."

"We're just kids," Angerman spoke up. His voice startled Teacher, he'd been so quiet for the last few hours. "Don't you guys get it? We're just kids. We shouldn't have to be taking responsibility for feeding ourselves, rationing, stuff like that."

Teddy Bear began to sniffle. Mommy draped an arm over his shoulders and wiped his nose with the tablecloth. "C'mon, it's okay," she whispered. "We'll figure this out." She glared at Angerman.

"But I'm thirsty," Teddy Bear whimpered.

Teacher sighed, let her eyes fall back to The Book. And realized, with a shock, that her right hand happened to be hovering over a passage on page 144 written in pencil:

> And he showed me a pure river of water of life, clear as crystal, proceeding from the throne of God and of the Lamb.

Teacher began to tremble with excitement. Surely this was a sign.

"I have received a message from The Book!" she announced. She read the passage to the others, felt herself reveling in each word. "The 'pure river of water of life.' It's gotta be a sign that the family should be traveling to Washington, District of Columbia, on a river. We'd have all the water we needed."

Angerman frowned. "River? That's nuts. There's no river 'round here."

"Must be," Teacher insisted. She began going through The Book, trying to find the maps.

Angerman came and hovered over her shoulder as she turned the rippled pages.

"Those maps, where are those maps?" she wondered, all impatience now. All of a sudden, she felt Angerman grab her wrist, hard. She winced in pain. "Ow! What're you doing?"

And then Teacher saw. Angerman had made her stop at That Page. The one with the kitty litter ad and the page torn from a puppy care manual. The one where she had found the words *Second* and *Coming* circled in pencil.

Angerman let go of her wrist and turned away. Then he began rushing around the room in some sort of mad panic, knocking down chairs, searching for something. The children watched him, speechless.

"What're you doing?" Teacher called out, rubbing her wrist. "Angerman, what's wrong with you?"

Angerman stopped and grabbed his picture frame which was propped up against Bad Guy. He held it up to his face. "Good evening! And now the news," he said in his Grown-up anchorman voice. His eyes were fiery and black in the candlelight, and he had that creepy smile on his face. "Today at the Alpenhaus Restaurant in Some Town, Florida, it was announced that—Where's my cue card? Oh, yes—Second helping. Second coming. And behold I am coming quickly, and My reward is with Me, to give to every one according to his work. No, no, no, no. The Panthers kicked the bejeesus out of the Angels last night, 666 to 3. Then the fourth angel poured out his bowl on the sun, and power was given to him to scorch men with fire. And men were scorched with great heat, and they blasphemed the name of God who has power over these plagues; and they did not repent and give Him glory."

After a shocked moment of silence, Teacher picked up her pencil and began writing in The Book, as fast as she could.

Hunter rose from his chair. "Angerman, stop it! You're scaring us."

Teacher waved her arm. "No, no, no," she cried out. "Keep going, we need to know this!"

Angerman pointed to Puppy and Kitty, who were clinging to each other at the table. "Congratulations! You have been chosen by our panel of judges to, to—No, it cannot happen! *CANNOT HAPPEN!* The President's New Deal helped Florida to recover from the Great Depression. A rod of iron, the scarlet beast. Sodom and Egypt. This is NOT EGYPT. This is Florida, just Florida. SOMEBODY PLEASE HELP US, WE'RE CHILDREN!"

Angerman cast the frame aside, sank to his knees, and buried his face in his hands. Mommy choked back a sob and ran over to him. Teacher watched them for a second, then continued writing in The Book. This was big, this was Big Information, she could feel it in her bones.

Angerman squinted against the morning light. It hurt his eyes, made it hard to pedal. They were going up a slight rise, past some dense woods scarred with grown-over forest fire damage, an occasional house. The Alpenhaus was far behind them. Soon they would hit a river, according to Teacher's map. And just past the river, the Interstate. Which was the route they'd agreed on over breakfast, over their tense, let's-keep-conversation-at-a-minimum breakfast.

It was quiet now, too. Just the sound of pedals, the steady whirring of gears. No one was talking, not even the little ones. He knew it was because of him, because of last night. They all thought he was crazy. Nuts. Out of his mind.

They didn't realize it, but this stuff was scary and confusing for him, too. He had no idea what came over him when he went off on these rants. No control. When he saw those words in Teacher's Book last night, it was like some demon entered his soul, poisoned it, set it on fire. Next thing he knew, he found himself speaking through the frame, shouting Those Words.

The family was right. He was a madman. A madman in a kid's body.

"Angerman?"

It was Mommy, addressing him through the flaps. He turned his head. "Yes? Are you okay back there? Was I going too fast?"

"I'm fine. Where are we now?"

Angerman glanced around. "Woods. They're pretty. Do you want to take a look?"

There was a long silence behind him. Angerman turned his head again. Mommy's hands crept out of the opening, parting the flaps a little. She poked her head out gingerly.

A wide smile spread across her face. "Look at those flower trees over there! Aren't they beautiful?"

Angerman looked. There was a cluster of pink cassia trees nestled among the azaleas, and a couple of ibises were wading through a swampy patch of ground. Large, green-spotted butterflies fanned their wings on the surface of a puddle.

"Yes, they're beautiful." Angerman felt himself breathe a little. "This reminds me of—"

"Of what?"

Angerman smiled and shook his head. "Dunno. A trip. Some trip. I don't remember, exactly. But it was a pretty place, like this."

"The river!"

Teacher's cry startled Angerman. He snapped his head around, faced forward. Everyone was talking suddenly: "River, river, river!"

Up ahead, just past a bend in the road, was a snakey stretch of golden-brown water. Was it the one on Teacher's map?

Angerman, who was third in the pack, pedaled even faster. If this really was the river, the Interstate was just on the other side over the bridge. Once they were on the Interstate, they would be able to make better speed to Washington. They had to get there as quickly as possible. It was scary and confusing to him that he knew this. But he did.

He rounded the bend behind Teacher—and slammed on his brakes. His bike came to an abrupt stop. "What happened?" Mommy cried out.

Angerman couldn't even bear to say.

The bridge over the river was washed out.

Chapter Fifteen

Mommy reached out to the zipper and opened the flap a hand's length.

"What's wrong?" she asked, poking just her eyes and nose into the opening.

Angerman was blocking her line of sight directly ahead, and to the left and right Teacher and Hunter were straddling their bikes while the younger children stood each with one foot on the ground. They were all looking ahead, up the road. Above their heads were horsetail clouds in a robin's-egg sky.

"What is it?" Mommy had to unzip the flap a little more and poke her head all the way out.

A dragonfly buzzed past, its enormous eyes blue-green in the sunlight. Hunter turned around to look at Mommy at last: the sunglasses he wore flashed and glinted, making her throw up one hand to ward off the glare. Without speaking, Hunter walked his bike out of her view, and Mommy glanced beyond him.

The river stretched across their path, hemmed in on either bank by masses of trees so thickly overgrown that it was hard to make out what they were—cypresses or water locusts or tupelos—and everything was tied and snarled together with vines and strangler figs. It reminded Mommy of that fairy story where a princess fell asleep and a wall of pricker bushes grew up around her castle, prickers so thick and tall that nobody could penetrate them. Above the wall of green riverside trees floated flocks of yellow butterflies, as if the leaves were giving off sparks. Their road stretched to the edge of the river. Little remained of the bridge but a narrow stretch of paved sections staggered across the water on rusty struts. It must have been damaged in a flood or horrorcane. Now it was obvious from one look that it could be walked, and bikes could be pushed—carefully. But it was also obvious that nothing wider than skinny kids and narrow bikes in single file would cross that bridge.

"What—how will we get the wagons over?" Mommy asked, her voice small.

Angerman's back was still to her, but Bad Guy stared at her. The gouges in his face were like the scratches of a giant cat. Mommy didn't want the screaming spirit to stand up inside her. She wished Bad Guy wouldn't look at her that way. In desperation, she pushed her shoulders out of the wagon and rose in an awkward crouch, half in and half out, looking back the way they had come. Heat rippled over the road, spreading mirages like puddles across the pavement.

"This is not good," Teacher said.

Hunter swung his leg over his bike and popped the kickstand, walking back to join Mommy. She knew he was coming, and knew what he was going to say, but she looked wildly around, looking for an alternative. Behind them, not far back, the road had forked away to the left, and she followed it with her eyes: in the distance, it entered a dark forest.

"Mommy, you're gonna have to—" Hunter began.

"Why can't we go that way?" she blurted, pointing at the far forest. "That road is going north—that's the way we want to go, right? Why can't we do that?"

She looked from Hunter to Teacher to Angerman. Their expressions were a mixture of pity and embarrassment and worry. Sun and exertion had brought red flushes to everyone's cheeks, and their hair was stuck to their foreheads with sweat. Mommy's hope slipped away from her like a minnow darting into shadow.

"You want to go through a forest?" Angerman scoffed. "Do you know what's in forests now?"

Mommy shrank back. "No."

He narrowed his eyes. "Poison snakes. Wild pigs with tusks." He leaned toward her, making Mommy shrink back even further, a turtle retreating into its shell. "Wild pigs can kill small children."

"How do you know?" Hunter demanded, moving closer to Mommy, protecting her.

Angerman's gaze flicked to Hunter's face. "I've seen it happen, that's how I know."

Mommy noticed the little ones staring, listening, and she felt a sour taste swarm up the back of her throat. "Who can pick me some pretty flowers?" she asked them with fake cheer. "Go on, get me some really pretty ones."

But Teddy Bear, Action Figure, Baby, and Doll didn't move. Their eyes were huge. Even Action Figure looked stunned and frightened at the thought of wild pigs.

"And that's not all," Angerman continued, his head swiveling from one to another as he spoke. "Panthers. Coyotes. Deadly spiders. Bears."

"Stop it!" Mommy clapped her hands over her ears.

But Angerman was relentless. "If you look across the river here, you can see that the road passes through that line of trees on the other side, but then it's clear. The road goes across open land—probably clear to the Interstate. At least we'd be able to see anything coming."

Teddy Bear pitched forward suddenly and threw up, his breakfast gushing out all over the cracked pavement. Doll and Baby both shrieked and sprang backward, tangling themselves in their bicycles. Flies immediately settled onto the vomit. Miserable Teddy Bear wiped his face with his shirtsleeve.

"Mommy, we can't go through that forest. We have to go this way, but we can't take the wagons over," Hunter said with an apologetic grimace. "You'll have to get out."

Sweat beaded on Mommy's upper lip and her scalp prickled. "Okay, okay," she whispered, gripping the edges of the bike wagon and feeling nothing more substantial to support her than flimsy nylon and a wobbly aluminum frame. She fixed her eyes on the end of the storm-wrecked bridge. It quivered in a heat distortion. "I can do it."

But she wasn't sure if she said it out loud, because the roaring in her ears was deafening.

Hunter breathed a sigh of relief. "Great, great." He patted Mommy's arm, feeling dumb but not knowing how else to comfort her. "Take your time."

"Not too much time," Angerman warned.

"Give her a break, man," Hunter said, frowning. He bent to tackle the nuts and bolts holding the wagon to his bike. "We gotta figure out how to do this, gotta ride Puppy and Kitty on handlebars . . ."

"And Mommy needs a bike," Teacher said.

Mommy was still trying to extricate herself from the wagon on Angerman's bicycle, pulling herself out as slowly as a hermit crab emerges from its shell after a shock. One leg. Then the other leg. Hunter had to turn away.

"Where's the tools?" he asked.

"Mommy will have to take Teddy's or Action's bike," Angerman announced. "The girls' bikes are too small for her."

"No way! Uh-uhn!" Action Figure pushed away, swinging himself onto the seat of his bike as he pedaled out of range. He stopped by the edge of the bridge, head lowered between his shoulders, glowering like a small bull.

"You can take my bike," Teddy Bear said, his face still ashen. "Mommy, you can take my bike. I can go with Teacher." But Mommy couldn't look at him. She was still struggling to master her fear.

Teacher had begun piling their supplies on the ground next to her bicycle, sloppy piles of clothes and stacks of food. Camping equiment. She wrestled the tent in its slippery duffel bag out of the wagon and tossed it into the weeds. It landed with a *whump* and a faint clank of tent poles. Hunter looked up from his work to see how Mommy was making it. There was a tap at his shoulder, and it was Angerman handing him the wrenches. Tapping him with the metal tools, not lightly, either.

"Come on, let's get this over with," Angerman said.

Hunter bit back his irritation and bent to his task while Baby coaxed Puppy and Kitty out of their wagon. As he worked, Hunter kept an eye on Angerman, who was readjusting his backpack to make more room for food and canteens, although it was obvious he wasn't going to ditch Bad Guy. Puppy and Kitty sat cross-legged on the road, holding hands, never looking away from Angerman. They ignored Baby, who fussed and cooed over them like a little mother. Hunter banged at the last bolt to pop it out, and the wagon's tie-bar dropped off the rear axle of his bike.

He stood, aware of the ache in his legs and back, but not caring, not minding, really. They were doing something. Going somewhere. With his sunglasses on everything was pretty clear, and he felt they could solve these problems. They had to solve these problems.

"Don't play near the edge of the river," he heard Teacher say.

At the end of the bridge, where the steep bank dropped twenty feet to the water, Doll and Action Figure were doing some kind of balancing contest, seeing who could stand on one leg longest. Hunter noted with relief that his brother was acting friendly and civilized, and then he bent to begin unhitching the wagon from Teacher's bike. He positioned himself to work where he could see Mommy and Angerman and the rest of them.

"Hunter?"

He looked over his shoulder. It was Teddy Bear.

"Hey, kiddo, do you feel better now?" Hunter asked, turning back to his tools. *Hey kiddo. Howya doin, kiddo.* Someone used to say that to him.

"Hunter, is there alligators down there?" Teddy Bear whispered.

Hunter stalled, pretending to concentrate on fitting the wrench around the silvery bolt. "Well, umm, I won't lie to you, Teddy. You're a big boy, so I'll be honest with you. There probably are alligators down there, but the thing is—" He gripped the handle and turned, feeling the resistance suddenly give way. "The thing is, we're going across the river, and so we won't come anywhere close to them. You'll be fine."

From the look on Teddy Bear's face, it was clear the boy wasn't nearly so sure. But he nodded gamely. His throat moved as he swallowed.

"Go help Teacher, okay?" Hunter said, shooing Teddy Bear away.

It was time to work on Angerman's bike. Hunter looked to see if Mommy had managed to get herself out into the open, and was relieved to see Mommy astride Teddy Bear's bike. Her eyes were closed; she wasn't going anywhere, just standing there with both feet planted on the ground and her fists wrapped tight around the handlebars. Angerman stood at her side, saying something into her ear in a low voice. The look on Angerman's face got Hunter to his feet with a jolt of fear. He strode over.

"What's going on here?" he demanded. "What were you saying to her?"

Mommy's face was pale and damp with sweat. Angerman was in one of his moods or trances or whatever that was that he did. The moment Hunter grabbed him by the shoulder, Angerman turned away, turning Bad Guy—strapped to his backpack—to Mommy and Hunter. A chill swept across Hunter's neck.

"You okay?" he asked Mommy.

She nodded, not opening her eyes.

"You have to try riding the bike," Hunter said.

"I know," she whispered.

"Just open your eyes. I'll hold on if you want—you won't fall," Hunter continued. He felt a catch in his throat. "Come on, you can do it. You have to try."

Mommy nodded again, but her eyes were still squeezed shut. She was breathing hard through her nose, and sweat was beading on her forehead like raindrops.

There was a crash, a bike being thrown to the ground. Angerman stalked over to confront Mommy.

"If you don't ride that bike we're going to leave you here," he said, his eyes wild. "Get moving!"

"Shut up!" Hunter yelled.

"Make that bicycle move!" Angerman shouted, inches away from Mommy's ear. "Open your eyes and MOVE!"

"I can't do it!" Mommy screamed. "I can't do this!"

Hunter drew his arm back to hit Angerman, shove him away, but there was a cry from the end of the bridge.

"Dolly!"

Mommy's eyes flew open. Hunter began running, terrible thoughts flying through his head even as he saw that Teddy Bear, Action Figure, Baby—and Doll—were all there, standing looking over the edge. But Doll was sobbing, pounding her fists against Action Figure.

"What happened?" Hunter called as he ran.

"Alligators!" Teddy Bear said.

At that, Doll began to scream, shrieking as though she were being stuck with pins. Action Figure looked down the bank, eyes aglow.

Hunter followed Action Figure's gaze and saw Doll's dolly, far below in the water, floating downstream.

Doll's screams were horrible. Baby tried to put her arms around Doll, but it was no use. Teddy Bear was crying, too, and Hunter could hear Puppy and Kitty begin to cry as the commotion reached them, back with the others.

"Sinkin'!" Action Figure said and Doll screeched again.

Hunter grabbed his brother by both arms and shook him. "Did you do this? Did you do this?"

Without waiting for an answer, Hunter turned and began lowering himself over the edge.

Teacher reached the top of the bank just in time to see Action Figure go slithering down after Hunter. Doll was hysterical, coughing and sobbing. Teddy Bear was crying about alligators, and even Baby was beginning to wail.

"This is crazy!" Angerman shouted. "You're all slowing me down!"

"Don't cry," Teacher told the children, knowing it was a ridiculous thing to say to them. "Hunter will get the dolly."

"But an alligator could—"

"There are no alligators!" Teacher snapped.

Teddy Bear nodded, his head bobbing up and down. "Hunter said there was."

Teacher was torn between helping the children and needing to see what was happening with Mommy and Angerman. She took Teddy Bear and Baby by the hand, pulling them onto the ground to sit. "Say the Baby-Sees," she ordered, and hurried back to the others.

It was bad. Mommy was tearing her way into the wagon, the bike fallen where she had dropped it. Puppy and Kitty were whimpering, and Angerman was jabbing his elbows back at Bad Guy so hard it must have hurt him, but he didn't even wince.

"Stop it! Just leave her alone!" he was yelling.

With a shudder, Teacher turned away from Angerman and tried to grab Mommy's ankle before it disappeared into the little wagon. "Mommy, no!"

Mommy kicked and thrashed out of Teacher's grip, and her hand appeared, fumbling to zip the flaps shut. Teacher swatted at Mommy's hand and bent to poke her head in. Mommy was trying to curl herself into a ball.

"Don't do this," Teacher pleaded. "Mommy, don't

leave me. I can't do this by myself."

"Nonono," Mommy said, her hands over her face.

Teacher dropped her head for a moment, helpless. If she could look at The Book it would have answers, but there was no time, no time to get out The Book and study it the way she wanted to. She had to do something now. She could still hear the little ones crying and wailing.

"Just leave me here, leave me behind, it's okay, I'll be okay," Mommy was saying. "It doesn't matter. I can't do anything anyway."

"Don't say that!"

"It's true! I'm no use to anyone!"

Teacher grabbed Mommy's hands and dragged them away from her face. "You have to help me. I can't make the little ones stop crying. They don't listen to me. How do I make them stop crying?"

"I don't—"

"No!"

Teacher froze. That was Teddy Bear's voice.

"Don't go!" he cried out. Then more urgently: "Teacher!"

She backed out of the wagon, the zipper tearing at her hair. When she whirled around to see what was happening, she saw Angerman, with Bad Guy strapped to his back, dragging Puppy and Kitty across the bridge.

Chapter Sixteen

As Hunter made his way down the steep bank, he could feel mud swarming, oozing around his ankles. Like how he had always imagined it would be to walk through quicksand. He angled his body, kept his knees bent, grabbed at branches, cattails, anything to keep from slipping. Below, he could see Doll's dolly spinning in the current, arms spread out like a Christmas angel against the murky brown water. Traveling north.

Above him, the vines and strangler figs were so dense that he could no longer make out the others up on the road. He could hear the muffled sounds of the little ones shrieking and sobbing.

He could see, under the bridge, some spray-painted words: GRIFFIN + CHELSEA 4-EVER.

Cicadas hummed in the heat, bullfrogs twanged. A great blue heron swelled up from a rotting log, its wings flapping in slow motion through the thick air. Through Hunter's new sunglasses, the sky looked hazy and yellow.

Almost at the bottom now.

"Where'dit go, where'dit go?"

Hunter's head whipped around. Action Figure was half running, half sliding down the muddy bank, bow and arrow in hand. His cheeks were flushed bright pink, and he was panting, grinning with excitement.

"Action, this is all your fault!" Hunter scolded him.

"You dropped the dolly in the river on purpose, didn't you?"

Action Figure wouldn't look at him. "Could rescue it with my bone arra," he offered, scoping the river.

"Go on back with the others," Hunter snapped. "Just go."

Without waiting for a reply, Hunter continued to the edge of the river. Where did the dolly go? He had taken his eyes off it for a minute while he and Action Figure were talking. The current was fast—perhaps the thing had washed away altogether. He clenched his fists, annoyed with himself. A good hunter never let himself lose sight of his prey.

Then—there it was, just below him, tangled up in a carpet of stringy weeds and plastic wrappers and a brown beer bottle. Its one free arm was batting back and forth in the current, and its one good eye was gazing up at the sky.

Hunter knew he had to get to it fast, before it got loose and floated away. He slid down to the weeds, leaned over a brambly bush, and dipped his hand into the sun-dappled river. The water was warm, mossy feeling. He gripped his fingers around the dolly, yanked it out of the weeds, hauled himself upright. Mission accomplished.

There was a splashing sound. Action Figure had followed him to the bottom and was ankle-deep in water. He was poking at weeds and litter with the tip of his arrow, stirring up the muck.

Hunter ignored him and started back up the bank with the soaking-wet dolly.

Then something caught his eye.

Something was happening up on the bridge. It was Angerman. Angerman was going across the bridge with the Bad Guy mannequin strapped to his backpack and dragging Puppy and Kitty behind him by their hands. The wild ones were struggling a little but not much.

At the edge of the bridge, Teacher was waving her arms at Angerman and yelling something. Hunter couldn't hear what. But Angerman didn't look back at her, just kept picking his way—a patch of pavement here, a rusty strut there—toward the other side. Pure determination.

Tucking the dolly under his arm, Hunter cupped his hands over his mouth and shouted: "Angerman!"

No response.

Hunter exhaled sharply. What was going on? He grabbed a bunch of cattails, using them to hoist himself up and over a large rock. It was the fastest way up.

"Wait, come wit you!" Action Figure cried out. Hunter turned. His brother swung his arms behind him for momentum like a bird, and jumped up onto the bank.

But he lost his foothold. Hunter watched in horror as Action Figure slipped in the mud and fell forward. Arms flailing, feet flying out from under him, head about to smash into the rock.

Without even thinking, Hunter threw himself down on top of the rock to cushion the blow. He felt his brother's head collide against his arm: a mad tangle of hair, skin, limbs.

Action Figure lay still for a moment—half against the rock, half against Hunter's body, just breathing heavily—then wriggled, scrambled to his feet. He stared at Hunter, his green eyes enormous. Then he blinked and turned and began sloshing up the muddy bank, fists in the air. "Lessgo, lessgo!" he demanded.

Hunter rubbed his arm where Action Figure's head had collided with it. Then he picked up the dolly, which had fallen to the ground, and ran up the bank after him.

Some crisis had happened while he and Action Figure were down at the river. At the top of the road, Mommy was clinging to the railing of the bridge, sobbing and shrieking. Knuckles white, knees buckling, face drenched in sweat. She looked like a crazy person.

"Angerman!" she screamed. "Angerman, you bring those babies back, do you hear me?"

Hunter glanced over. Angerman and the wild ones were on the other side of the bridge, almost out of sight.

Doll, Baby, and Teddy Bear were squatting down on the dirt road, their fists curled against their faces, sobbing. Teacher was patting their heads, trying to comfort them. "Shh, it's okay. Angerman's just taken Puppy and Kitty for a little walk."

"DO YOU HEAR ME, ANGERMAN?" Mommy screamed at the top of her lungs.

"Mommy, stoppit!" Baby moaned through her fists. "Stop yelling like that!"

Hunter ran up to Teacher. "*What* is going on? What happened?"

She stared up at him, her eyes full of desperation. "We've gotta do something. He's taken the strays."

"Why?"

"I think he thinks he's taking them to Washington all

by himself. I think he thinks we were slowing him down or something. Shh, Teddy," she murmured, patting the boy's head.

Hunter gritted his teeth. He always knew Angerman was out of his mind. This was proof—as if the mannequin and the picture frame and the wild, raving speeches weren't bad enough. How far did he think he would get with the wild ones to take care of, with hardly any food and no fresh water at all? What did he know about taking care of children, anyway?

Action Figure came running up to Hunter. "Goin' with Angerman!" he announced.

"You are *not* going with Angerman!" Hunter hissed. He thrust the water-soaked dolly at Doll. "Here. I got her for you outta the river. Stop crying!"

"T-t-t-thank y-y-y-ou," Doll blubbered, taking the doll from him and clutching it to her chest.

Mommy let out a horrible wail. Hunter's head shot up. On the far side of the bridge, Angerman and the wild ones were rounding a bend in the road. A moment later, they disappeared from view.

"NOOOOOOO," Mommy sobbed. She let go of the railing and began shuffling, staggering back to the covered wagon. "They're gone, they're gone, they're gone," she moaned.

Hunter narrowed his eyes. It was obvious what had to be done. "They're not gone, I'll go after them," he told Mommy and Teacher.

Teacher frowned. "You can't go alone. He's—It's too dangerous. Besides, he won't come back, and he won't give up the strays, either."

Mommy stopped and turned. "You two go. I'll—I'll

stay here with the children."

"Mommy," Hunter said. "You're in no shape—"

"I'll be fine," Mommy said, swiping at her tearstained face with the back of her hand. "Please, just go. Bring them back safe. Who wants a snack?" she called out to the little ones, her voice high and bright.

Hunter gave her a doubtful look, but Teacher tugged at his arm. "Come on. Before they get too far."

Action Figure looked up at Hunter. Hunter shook his head. "No. You stay here with Mommy. She and the others need you to protect them."

Action Figure made a face, then joined Mommy and the little ones at her covered wagon. Hunter turned to Teacher. "Okay, let's go get them."

Mommy was having a hard time breathing. Her breath felt shallow in her chest, and her face was hot and cold at the same time. Waves, waves of nausea and dizziness, like she was going to pass out any second, like she was being washed away into darkness. How would she get through the next second, the next minute, the next hour? She wanted to crawl into her wagon and curl up in a ball. Tuck her fists under her chin, close her eyes, just let herself disappear and become a nothing.

But she couldn't. Baby, Doll, and Teddy Bear had followed her into the wagon, cramming inside and crawling into her lap, tugging on her shirt. She could see that they were terrified.

"Dolly wants to know, where's Angerman gone to?" Doll asked her in a tiny voice.

"You tell Dolly not to worry. He's coming back," Mommy reassured her.

"Wild pigs," Teddy Bear whispered.

"There're no wild pigs over in that forest, Teddy. Angerman was just making up stories," Mommy said. "Speaking of stories, who wants to hear a story? Not a scary story but a happy story?" The children dabbed at their eyes and waved their hands in the air, crying, "Me, me, me!"

Action Figure was standing at the end of the bridge, watching Teacher and Hunter go. Hearing the other children, he turned and came over to the wagon. He hoisted his bow off his shoulders, hunkered down, and climbed in onto the pile without a word.

Mommy ruffled his hair, which was matted with burrs and dead leaves. "Snack and story time, Action. I think we have—let's see—" She began rooting through her pockets. "How 'bout some gum?"

"Yesssss!" Baby said, reaching out a hand.

"Okey-dokey then." Mommy went through the motions of dividing up the snacks. *Four children, rip two pieces of gum in half.* Her hands shook, and she dropped one of the halves into the tangle of laps. She bit her lip, trying not to cry out in frustration. Everything had been so much easier in Lazarus. Out here, out in the open, it took everything out of her just to perform the simple task of feeding her children.

Action Figure pounced on the wayward gum and shoved it in his mouth. "Whassa story?" he demanded.

"Once upon a time," Mommy began, "there was a girl named—um—" She searched her memory. What, *what* was that fairy tale she loved so much? Someone used to tell it to her every night before she went to bed. "Cindy Ella. Cindy Ella lived with a mean Mommy who wasn't her First Mommy, and two sisters who were really mean to her, too. They made her clean and cook all the time. They wouldn't let her leave the house."

Baby stared at her with wide eyes. "You're a Mommy, and you're not mean."

"This is a scary story," Doll complained.

"No, honey, it's a *happy* story," Mommy insisted, handing her a piece of gum. "Because a wonderful, kind Fairy Gobmother came to Cindy Ella one day and helped her leave the house and her mean Mommy and sisters. The Fairy Gobmommy made a beautiful dress for Cindy Ella so she could go to a fancy party. And the Fairy Gobmommy made Cindy Ella a, um, big giant wagon out of pumpkins, so she could get to the party."

"A wagon outta pumpkins!" Teddy Bear said in wonder. "What's pumpkins?"

"Was Angerman pulling the wagon?" Doll asked her.

"No, horses," Mommy replied. "Four beautiful, strong horses."

The children chewed their gum in silence. Mommy's eyes wandered to the bridge and the road beyond. Her throat tightened, and she tried hard not to start crying again.

Listening to the bullfrogs twanging, to a lone seagull screeching in the bright blue sky, Mommy tucked her chin into her knees and prayed for a Fairy Gobmommy to come save her. Save them all.

Teacher kicked a dead branch that was lying in the path. "They couldn't have gotten far. They had ten minutes on us, tops."

"We should never've let him into the house that night

he showed up," Hunter muttered.

Yes, we should've, Teacher wanted to say. She knew deep down, she knew in her bones, that despite everything, Angerman was meant to join their family. According to The Book, his presence was part of some Big Plan.

But she made herself keep still. She could see from Hunter's face, could tell from the edge in his voice, that he was in a state about Angerman. That he hated him.

An osprey cried out from the top of a cypress tree. The air was hot and damp and thick with the smell of wild orchids. Teacher wiped a bead of sweat from her forehead. Where were they? Surely, Angerman couldn't have made much progress with that awful mannequin on his back and dragging the two strays.

"Could've stopped him, if I hadn't had to get that dolly for Doll," Hunter complained.

"The dolly." Teacher stopped in her tracks. "Current was carrying it away, wasn't it?"

Hunter nodded. He considered a moment. "Yeah. North. Why?"

"North," Teacher repeated. Her heart hammered in her chest. "Hunter, The Book! The message from last night, remember? 'The pure river of water of life.' I said it then—we're meant to travel to Washington on a river."

Hunter started. "You think *this* is the river?"

"Could be," Teacher said, her voice swelling with excitement. "Now that I think of it, rivers flow into the ocean. Maybe if we could take this river north, it would eventually empty out into the Atlantic. And we could find some road along the coast to get us to Washington. In the meantime, we'd have all the fresh water we needed."

Hunter nodded. "Maybe. Maybe. All we'd have to do is—well, find some boats. And Puppy and Kitty, of course."

Teacher made a face at him. "Angerman, too."

Hunter shrugged.

Just then, they heard a faint banging sound through the trees. *Bang, bang, bang.* Regular and rhythmic. And then, a second later, a loud, anguished cry.

Teacher and Hunter glanced at each other, then broke into a run. The sound was getting louder now. Teacher tried to keep from thinking: *wild pigs, panthers, alligators.* She gasped for breath, made herself run even faster as she and Hunter entered a thick grove of banyan trees.

At the far edge of the grove, Angerman was pummeling Bad Guy with a rock, over and over again on its chest. *Bang, bang, bang.* Nearby, Puppy and Kitty were huddled on the ground, clutching each other. Just staring, staring at Angerman as he tried to beat Bad Guy to death.

Chapter Seventeen

Mommy smoothed Doll's hair back from her forehead. The inside of the wagon was hot and becoming stuffier and steamier with each breath they drew, and the children were sleepy with it. Doll shifted her position, digging her head into Mommy's lap. Baby was lying on her side, tracing a pattern on the nylon wall of the tent with her finger and murmuring the Baby-Sees song. Teddy Bear was lying down, too, his eyes half closed. Even Action Figure, sitting cross-legged on everybody's feet, nodded and swayed. Even as Mommy glanced at him, he let himself down and sprawled, almost drunk with heat and sleepiness. The sun beating down on the nylon covering of the wagon was as heavy as a hand pressing them into the ground.

"Do you remember the story about the magic beans?" Mommy said, more to herself than to them. She licked her lips. "There was a boy named Jack who had some magic beans, and he planted them. They turned into a beanstalk that went high, high, high, and so they also called it a Woodstock and everyone was happy. Then George came and chopped it down. His First Daddy said, 'Did you chop that down, George?' and George said, 'I cannot lie down,' so they made him President. The President is supposed to be awake all the time, see, and watch over all the children so they're safe."

Teddy Bear stirred. "Is that the President we're going to find?"

A wiggle of doubt crept into Mommy's memory, and her fingers stopped their nervous stroking through Doll's hair. "I don't think so. I think he was a different one. But his name was Washington, so maybe it is. No wait, that's the name of where President lives." She shook her head. "I just can't remember, Teddy."

"I'm thirsty," mewed Baby.

"Me, too," Doll said.

Mommy looked at Action Figure, knowing she was a coward. He was sleeping the hard, heavy sleep of children, and Mommy knew it would be despicable of her to wake him up and send him for water. She combed her fingers through Doll's hair again. "Shh, they'll be back soon and we'll have some water."

"But I'm thirsty now," Baby whined. "I'm hot."

"They'll be back soon," Mommy said again, wondering if they would be back at all. "Can't you wait?"

Baby rolled onto her back and stared up at the ceiling, which cast a feverish red glow over her face. If it weren't for the slow rise and fall of her chest, she would have looked dead. Mommy eased Doll off her lap and extricated herself from the tangle of bodies.

"I'll get it—I'll get some water," she whispered.

If she did one thing at a time, just concentrated on one thing at a time, maybe she'd be able to do it. The first thing to do was unzip the flaps. She kept her eyes focused on her hand pulling down the zipper.

Next, she had to check out the situation just outside the wagon, where their gear and equipment were scattered. She bent forward and worked her head and shoulders out. The sun hit her hard. Sweat prickled on her scalp.

What if they didn't come back?

From the corner of her eye, Mommy saw an armadillo waddling down the side of the road, snuffling among the weeds. She turned her head to watch it disappear into a clump of myrtle that was tangled with passionflower vines. The flowers shook and shivered as the animal barged through.

Mommy drew a deep breath. There was a rope, just to her left, draped over a pile of clothes. If she just leaned out a little farther she'd be able to grab it. She crept forward, stretching out one hand, and had the rope. She ducked back into the shelter of the wagon, her heart racing. The little vehicle wobbled on its wheels.

"Did you get some water?" Doll asked.

"Not yet, sweetie. Just give me a minute."

If she was ever going to be any good to these children, Mommy knew she had to get out, get over it, get the water. For a moment she sat, squeezing the hank of rope in her hands, and then in one clumsy lunge, pushed herself all the way outside.

They have to come back. They can't leave us here.

She was on her hands and knees on the ground, with grit and pebbles digging into her skin. Next to Teacher's bike was their cooking gear. Keeping her eyes on the big pot, Mommy stood up and began walking. One foot and then the other. She stooped to pick up the aluminum pot, and fumbled the end of the rope around the handle, tying it in a sloppy knot.

White egrets picked their way among the grasses in a

field to the left. On the right a two-trunked pine tree stretched up to a sky streaked with clouds. In front, the road ran to the river and the broken bridge. Mommy's grip on the rope and the pot tightened, and her knuckles went white. She walked forward, staggering like someone whose legs have fallen asleep. Her skin prickled and itched as though ants crawled inside her clothes. A strange sound reached her ears, and she knew it came out of her mouth. There was another odd scraping sound, and that was her feet shuffling along the rough pavement.

But something could happen. If Teacher and Hunter can't find Angerman. Or if he does something crazy.

At the end of the bridge Mommy stopped to gather herself, as though she had just completed the first long leg of a difficult journey. The river below meandered off to the right and left between its thickly grown banks. Sunlight picked out little eddies and currents and the places where a log or a submerged tree stump and the broken pieces of the bridge decking divided the flow. The water was dark, and occasionally a leaf or stick drifted by, turning slowly. Mommy reached for the guardrail, mesmerized by the dark current, and took one shaky step out onto the bridge.

A movement caught her eye, and she followed it upward, a bird shooting up out of the foliage and vanishing in the glare of the sun. Dizzy, Mommy looked down again, and caught herself swaying. She grabbed the rail, breathing hard through her nose, and then slowly, slowly, began lowering the cookpot on its rope toward the dark, flowing current. It banged and bounced against the struts of the bridge as it descended. Then it caught on something.

They won't come back. Something terrible has happened.

Mommy twitched the rope as tears sprang to her eyes. She could feel the pot was caught on something, but she couldn't lean out over the water to see what it was. With a gasp, she jerked and yanked the rope, and then the rope went taught again, sliding through her hands. The pot hit the water below, and then the river caught it, tipping it over and pulling it beneath the bridge. Mommy began drawing it back, praying that the pot was actually filling with water and not just bobbing empty on the surface.

It was heavy. She could feel the heaviness of the water in the pot, and laughed a harsh, breathless laugh, pulling hand over hand to bring it up again. The rope twirled and spun, and she heard the pot go *thunk* against the understructure of the bridge. Faster and faster she pulled, and the rope slithered in a heap at her feet. She risked leaning out over the guardrail, and there was the pot, just within reach, sparkling wet and full of clear water.

Mommy let out another half laugh, half sob, and grabbed the wire handle. Her hands trembled as she picked at the knot. For a moment she had to rest the pot on the ground, and then it was free, and she was running as fast as she could without spilling the water, back to the red wagon, back to safety.

Just as she ducked inside, she heard a call from the distance. She looked back over her shoulder. At the far end of the bridge were Teacher, and Hunter, and behind them were Angerman with Puppy and Kitty. All of

Mommy's muscles went limp, and she collapsed as the children began lapping at the pot of water.

Hunter took his turn to drink from the pot after they'd let Puppy and Kitty have as much as they wanted. He saw Mommy looking from him to Teacher to Angerman, a question in her eyes. He also saw Teacher meet her look and shake her head, as if to say, never mind, it's over, we're here.

"Okay," Hunter said, wiping water from his chin as he passed the nearly empty pot to Angerman. "We've got a new plan. We have to find some boats."

"I seen a boat," Action Figure said, pointing upstream. "Ovadere."

They all turned. Hunter's eyes took a moment to adjust to the new distance as he looked through the sunglasses. Upstream, where the river bent out of sight, were the remains of a rotted dock; and back among the trees, there was a glimpse of a sagging roofline.

"It's a cabin," Angerman said.

"Let's go." Hunter took the lead, always glad to have a clear goal, to see his way clear. He and Angerman, with Action Figure prowling ahead, scrambled through the dense brush. Branches clawed at them as they pushed their way along the bank. Spears of sunlight shot down through openings in the leaves overhead. Action Figure hooted a warning.

"Gator!"

Hunter and Angerman stopped, waiting, and they heard the slithering splash as the alligator pushed off the mud and into the water. Action Figure's face glowed with excitement as he looked back at them through the trees. "C'mon. Cabin's here."

One last thicket of bushes with large, dark, leathery leaves stood between them and the dock. Angerman grunted as he turned around and backed through the branches, letting them scrape across Bad Guy's bashed face. With one arm raised to protect himself from the whipping twigs, Hunter followed. They didn't need to talk about what had happened back there on the road, how Teacher and Hunter had each picked up a child and started back, and Angerman had followed without a word, strapping Bad Guy to his back again. That was over, and Angerman and Puppy and Kitty had come back.

They burst out into a clearing. Action Figure stood on the last remaining plank of a dock that leaned at a crazy angle toward the water. Sunlight turned Action Figure's hair into a white halo, and the boy held both arms out, as if saying behold!

A canoe and a wide-bottomed bass boat were tied to the dock. The metal bass boat was underwater, pressed against the pilings by the current, and the back end was partly sunk in the mud. The canoe was also full of water but it had enough buoyancy to stay afloat just below the surface. A brown fish was idling in the water beneath the forward thwart of the canoe, its tail swishing back and forth. The ropes that held both boats to the dock were nearly worn through.

"We'll have to get these out onto shore and empty them first and clean them out," Hunter said, his mind clicking through the tasks ahead of them. "Action, go see if there's any paddles or oars or anything in the cabin. Watch out for snakes."

Twigs and branches snapped as Action Figure headed up to the fishing shack. Hunter looked at Angerman. "Let's get the canoe out first."

Angerman was subdued and quiet, seeming ready to agree to Hunter's leadership for a while. What had happened back on the road would remain behind them. As the two boys worked, wading up to their waists in the water to wrestle the boats out, Hunter gave directions and Angerman followed them. The canoe was easy to drag out and overturn, and they left it on the bank, with streams of water following them as they sloshed back into the river. Churned mud turned the water murky as they rocked the bass boat back and forth to loosen it. Swampy gas bubbled up, and a swarm of wiggling larvae suddenly bobbed up on the surface of the water before the current whisked them away.

At last the bass boat came free, and Hunter and Angerman dragged it in jerking stages up onto shore. Hunter's shoulders ached with the strain of hauling the water-filled boat up the sloping, muddy bank. Angerman began sloshing water out over the sides with both hands, trying to lighten the load. Hunter joined him. They were both soaked to the skin already, and their feet squished inside their sneakers. At last the boat was bailed out enough so that they could tip it on its side, dumping the rest of the water. They stood for a moment, catching their breaths, watching the water drain away.

"Action!" Hunter called out. "Found anything?"

There was a brief pause before Action Figure's voice drifted out of the cabin. "Ya!"

There was a slap of a screen door, and Action

Figure's footsteps crackling through the underbrush. He appeared in a moment, carrying two canoe paddles under one arm. He was chewing.

"You found something to eat?" Angerman asked.

Action Figure put his free hand over his mouth and swallowed. His eyes were furtive. "No."

Angerman raised his eyebrows. "But you're—"

"Never mind," Hunter said, turning away. "Let's get back to work."

Once they had finished sloshing both boats clean of mud and dead leaves, Hunter and Angerman maneuvered them back close to the dock for launching. More searching in the mildewy, cobwebby cabin turned up oars with oarlocks attached, more rope, and slightly rusty fishing tackle. They pushed their new craft back into the water alongside the sagging dock, and tied them together. Then they loaded the oars and paddles and fishing gear, and shoved off. The two boats glided out onto the river, turned, and pointed themselves downstream.

"This is great!" Hunter said, stripping off his wet shirt and letting it fall in a sodden mass into the canoe. He picked up a paddle. He had a dim memory of *camp*. There was something in the Before Time called *Summer camp with water safety and canoe races*. His arms remembered how to hold the paddle and how to turn it. Swirls of water spun away from the paddle as he drew it back, and fish rose to examine the chain of drops that fell as he reached forward for another stroke. His heart lifted. They were going to the ocean. The river would take them right to it.

As they neared the bridge, the boys steered the boats

back toward the bank. Teacher and Teddy Bear and the other children stood at the top, their faces in shadow from the sun behind their heads. A voice inside Hunter said, *we're going to be okay*, and he felt the hull of the canoe bump softly against the bank, and there his family was, scrambling down to meet the boats, their voices high and excited like children going on a ride.

Chapter Eighteen

Teacher pulled the oar through the heavy water. Out of the corner of her eye she watched Hunter—who was doing the same thing on the other side of the wide-bottomed bass boat—and tried to imitate his motions precisely. She had never used oars before, not that she could remember, anyway. It was hard, painful work. The knobs of her shoulders ached, her forearms burned, sweat poured down her back. And yet there was something about the rhythm and steadiness of it—the repetition of pull, glide, lift—that she found comforting. She craned her head around to see where they were going: it would take some time to get used to facing backward while rowing.

The blue tent was facing her, stretched across the back of the boat. Hunter had come up with the idea to rig it for Mommy, to make her a little floating house. Through the tent walls, Teacher could hear Mommy's soft, singsongy voice. She was telling the strays and the girls a story about someone named George Woodstock, his famous cherry pies, his big tall hat.

A sudden breeze kicked up, making the tent walls tremble and flutter. *Like the sound of the flag on the flagpole at Allamanda Elementary School.*

The other boat, the canoe, glided up alongside them silent as an alligator. Teacher glanced over. Angerman was up front, paddling on his knees, his face flushed red. He had tied his long, curly brown hair back with a piece of old rope. Action Figure was paddling in back. Teacher was surprised at how strong the boy was, how steady his strokes. He was thriving on this journey.

Teddy Bear was in the middle, his hands wedged tight between his knobby knees, his eyes darting from left to right as they passed alligators sunning themselves on the riverbanks. Teacher smiled at him, but he wouldn't even look at her.

The top of Bad Guy's head was just visible over the side of the canoe. Teacher could make out one flat amber eye, one scratched-up cheek, one half of its crazy murderous smile.

Sunlight filtered through the branches overhead, making pools of shadow. They didn't talk very much, just looked around at the dense walls of green that hemmed them in. In a backwater beneath a mossy tree that sagged out from the bank, a manatee lolled as it grazed on water hyacinths. Teacher was about to point it out to the children, but then decided not to, in case Teddy Bear believed it was really an alligator.

"Can we take a break soon?" Mommy called from the tent. "Girls're getting hungry."

Hunter craned around and surveyed the river ahead. "Maybe that rock up there. We can stop and have sumpin to eat."

He pointed the nose of the bass boat toward a large, flat gray rock just ahead of them and to the right. There were willowy shrubs clustered all around it, providing shade from the morning sun. Teacher could already feel the cool of it. She let out a little sigh, and rowed faster.

They docked the boats. Hunter checked for alligators. "All clear!" he announced.

The children clambered onto the rock. "Careful, don't slip!" Mommy called from inside the tent.

Teacher figured Mommy wasn't coming out. She pressed her mouth to the tent wall and murmured, "Can you find us some snacks, Mommy?"

"Uh-huh, no problem," came Mommy's reply.

There were rustling noises and the sharp *zzzzz* of a zipper being unzipped, and then Mommy began passing things through the opening of the tent: dried beef, peanut butter, spoons, juice boxes. Teacher took them from her and handed them to Hunter and Angerman, who were already up on the rock.

The boys distributed the food to the little ones. Teacher was about to join them, but then changed her mind. She reached for her pillowcase, which she had kept near her feet all morning, and pulled The Book from it. She climbed out of the bass boat, being careful not to make it tip, and up onto the rock.

She leaned against the gnarled trunk of a tree, away from the others, and stretched her legs in front of her. The rock was pleasantly cool and damp against her skin. She rested The Book on her lap and started turning the thick pages. She remembered that she had taken some notes in the middle of the night. She couldn't remember what they were, though.

There was her writing, scratchy and purple, on page 194. Across a brochure for Ocala Riverboat Tours:

SEE REAL-LIVE MANATEES!

Hunter, Action, and Angerman found us boats today. We're going to start down the river at

first light. We found us a house to camp in, it's
like a shack with two rooms and like some First
Daddy used to fish here but not much else. It's
late now, everyone's asleep.
We're going to try to get to the ocean on this
river, this pure river of water of life. Plenty
of fresh water to drink, and we can catch fish
to eat and cook em on sticks.

LET CAPTAIN BILL SHOW YOU THE WONDERS OF FLORIDA!

Why can't I sleep I am so tired so tired so
tired. Angerman tried to take the strays to
Washington all by himself, Hunter and me had
to go after em. He was meant to come to us, I
know You have told us that, but more and more
it seems he is just plain crazy. Out of his mind.
We need a sign.

ADULTS $13.50 CHILDREN $6.50

Crying, someone's crying. Teddy is having a
Bad Dream.
Must go write it down.

AGGILLATOR NONONONONONO AGGILLATOR
DON'T TAKE HER MOMMY DADDY WHERE ARE
U THE AGGILLATORS TAKING THE BABY IT'S
TAKING THE BABY AWAY IT'S GOING TO EAT
HER UP WHERE ARE U?

Teacher slammed The Book shut. She felt the breath whoosh out of her, felt her chest go icy cold. The baby. The baby being dragged away by an alligator.

He used to call it that, her little brother. He used to call alligators aggillators.

Her head was heavy as stone as she made herself look up at Teddy Bear. He was on the other side of the big gray rock, gnawing at a piece of jerky while Baby and Doll combed his hair with twigs.

Their eyes met. His were like a little animal's, all bright and scared. Teacher wanted to say something, to call out to him. She could feel her mouth forming an O, but no sound came out.

"GOOD AFTERNOON! And now the news.

"We're here with a live report from the— What's this river called? Mississippi, Hudson, Ohio, Potomac, Seine, Thames, Nile, Ganges? Heck, let's just call it River X. Anyway, folks, we're here with a live report from River X, on board the S.S. *Yucky Old Bass Boat* and the S.S. *Canoe Full of Dead Bugs*.

"Last night the crew camped out in some two-room shack, and all was swell. We found a coupla candy bars in the cupboards, two big ole candy bars, which we split ten ways. That bread and fishes trick works every time.

"This morning, we started down River X on our Rockin' Party Flotilla to Our Nation's Capital. Yes! We're having a good time here. I believe Mommy's in a fetal position in her blue tent and Teddy Bear's crying about alligators again. We should be in Washington in, oh, three months, six months tops. We'll be bringing you live reports all along the way. Count on Channel 18 for the News That Matters to You!

"Did I mention the scenery? Very pretty stuff. Wild flowers, big blue herons, turtles, families of deer. Action Figure keeps wanting to hunt the baby deer with his bow and arrow, but he can't shoot real straight yet. Keep practicing there, young Action! Hey, is that a bobcat sleeping on that sunny branch up there? Yes, folks! It is. Kitty, take a lookee!

"Puppy and Kitty just came crawling out of Mommy's tent. Puppy, Kitty, can you tell the folks out there what you think of the Party Flotilla?

"'Woof,' says Puppy. 'Meow,' says Kitty. Translation: 'We think it's awesome!'

"WHAT?

"Shut up, you monster, or I'll wring your plastic neck!

"Sorry, folks, just a technical difficulty. Do not adjust your set.

"It's getting near evening now, so we'll be stopping soon to pitch camp. We've seen a lot of cabins and shacks along the way today, so that should be no problemo. We'll dock the boats and bring in the supplies, chase out the snakes and other critters. Then we'll catch some fish for dinner, roast them over an open fire. Maybe sing some campfire songs, like what's that one—'Hail to the Thief.' Ahh, the camping life. Nothing to complain about.

"Except— This just in! A live weather report. A tornado watch is in effect for Fairfield and Koreshan counties. Storm clouds are gathering."

Hunter sat down at the wooden table and bent over Teacher's maps. It was dark now and difficult to see. His sunglasses were no good to him at night, and the oil lamp wasn't much help; they couldn't make it work right, and it smoked a lot. The wooden chair creaked with the weight of him, and one of the legs made a snapping sound, threatening to break.

Behind him, Mommy and Angerman were trying to put the little ones to bed. But they weren't cooperating. They'd been cooped up in the boats all day, so they were restless, all stirred up. Baby and the wild ones were jumping up and down on the old couch, Baby chanting *"Jumpity, jumpity, jump!"* Teddy Bear had a long stick in his hand, and he kept going to each of the windows and looking out.

Action Figure was outside somewhere. Hunter could hear twigs snapping and breaking and the occasional *plop* of a stone being pitched into the river. He felt the familiar tightening in his chest—*what if panthers, what if alligators, what if what if what if?*—but he tried to ignore it, focus on the business at hand.

Doll was the only still one. She was sitting cross-legged on the floor of the old cabin, having a quiet, earnest conversation with her dolly.

Teacher came over and peered over his shoulder. "Can you tell where we are?"

Hunter glanced down at the maps. He squinted, trying to make the shapes and lines sharpen into pattern, come to order. "This river's not on your maps, I don't think," he mumbled. "But we're going north, I'm pretty sure. That's a good thing."

"Dolly says she saw some people on the riverbank today," Doll announced.

"If we keep going on it, we've gotta reach the

ocean—don't you think?" Teacher said.

"I suppose so." Then Hunter whirled around in his chair. "What'd you say, Doll?"

"Dolly says she saw some big people on the riverbank today," Doll squeaked.

Mommy, who was trying to get Baby and the wild ones to stop their jumping and get into jamas, turned and stared at Doll. "What, honey? What do you mean your dolly saw big people?"

Doll held her dolly up to her ear for a second. She nodded yes, yes, yes, then said, "Dolly says big tall people. They were in their houses."

Hunter, Teacher, and Mommy exchanged glances. "Did *you* see the big tall people, Doll?" Teacher asked her.

"No, just dolly," Doll said in a tiny voice.

Just then, Teddy Bear rushed over to Doll and grabbed the dolly away from her. Doll scrambled to her feet. "No—what are you doing—give her back!" she yelped.

Teddy Bear began hitting the dolly with his stick. "My alligator is gonna eat up your dolly! He's gonna take her to the river and eat her up!"

"NOOOO!" Doll wailed, reaching for her dolly. "Give her back!"

"Teddy, stop it!" Teacher cried out.

Then Teddy Bear threw his alligator stick aside. "Bad gator, givum back the dolly!" he scolded the stick in a deep, Grown-up voice. He handed dolly back to Doll and smiled. "Here you go—here's your dolly back, safe and sound!"

Doll blinked at Teddy Bear in confusion. "You may never touch my dolly again, never," she told him. Then she retreated to the corner of the room, sat down on the floor, and began rocking her dolly in her arms. "Iss okay, iss okay," she crooned.

Teacher raced across the room, bent over Teddy Bear, and whispered something in his ear.

Suddenly, there was a terrible rumbling noise in the sky. Hunter stood up. "Thunder," he said. "Storm coming. We've gotta get the boats out of the water, or they'll be swamped. Angerman, Teacher, come on—we can get Action to help."

But Angerman wasn't listening. He went over to the heap of camping equipment near the couch and picked up his picture frame. He held it up to his face. "Good evening! And now the news," he said with an eerie smile.

"There's no time for that, Angerman, come on!" Hunter said in irritation. The windows flashed white for a second, then went dark again. Rain began falling, like a hail of bullets on the metal roof of the cabin.

The door banged open, and Action Figure stomped in. His white-blond hair was plastered to his forehead. "Big storm!" he announced with a grin. "Mebbe a horrorcane!"

Angerman continued talking through the picture frame. "Forecast: Rain!" he said. "Monday rain, Tuesday rain, Wednesday rain, Thursday rain, Friday rain, Saturday rain, Sunday end of the world. Thaaaaaat's right, folks! The Lord saw that the wickedness of humankind was great in the earth, and that every inclination of the thoughts of their hearts was only evil continually. And the Lord was sorry that he had made humankind on the earth, and it grieved him to his heart. So the Lord said, 'I will blot out from the earth the human beings I have created—people together with animals and creeping things and birds of the air, for I am sorry that I have made them. I am going to bring a flood of waters on the earth, to destroy from under heaven all flesh in which is the breath of life; everything that is on the earth shall die.' And all the fountains of the great deep burst forth, and the windows of the heavens were opened. The rain fell on the earth forty days and forty nights and forty days—"

Teacher ran over to Angerman and tried to snatch the picture frame from his face. "Angerman, stop it! We've gotta get the boats—come *on!*"

"Let go—you are interrupting a live news broadcast!" Angerman shouted at her, his big black eyes full of fury.

Teacher and Angerman struggled for the frame. Everyone was silent, just watching in horror. Thunder rumbled and exploded in the sky.

Hunter saw it coming. He started across the room toward them, but it was too late.

Angerman raised his free hand in the air, the way he did when he was about to hit Bad Guy. But instead, he smacked Teacher across her face.

There was a stunned silence, broken only by another crack of lightning. Hunter sprang forward and threw Angerman against the wall, pushing his forearm across Angerman's throat. He pressed hard.

"What do you think you're doing?"

Angerman looked horrified. "I didn't mean it. I'm sorry! Teacher, I'm sorry!" he choked out.

Teacher had her hand to her cheek and was turned away, her shoulders hunched.

"Teacher, are you okay?" Mommy asked. She ran across the room and put her arms around Teacher, rubbing her back.

"Yeah," Teacher mumbled.

Hunter felt Angerman trying to push him away. Hunter shoved Angerman aside with a look of disgust. If it were up to him, he'd drop Angerman overboard at the first chance, leave him behind to rot in this jungle with his crazy mannequin. "We've gotta get the boats in," he said. "Let's go."

Chapter Nineteen

The morning came clear, with a blue sky showing through the branches of the trees that crowded the house. Out on the porch and on every patch of ground were leaves and blossoms and twigs blown down in the storm. On the riverbank, the boats were splattered with mud. A swift current ripped past the landing, carrying more leafy debris. Angerman kicked a branch off the bottom step of the porch. Behind him he could hear the chatter and bustle of the others making ready to depart.

"Look out," Hunter said to him, stepping out the front doorway with the packed up tent in one hand and a full backpack in the other. He didn't meet Angerman's eyes.

I want—please let me explain—I have to—Angerman wanted to say, but he didn't, only watched Hunter stride down to the boats, his feet crunching over twigs as he went. Angerman could feel Hunter's distrust and his worry pushing against him like heat radiating off asphalt. That was how Hunter was, protecting his family, looking out for danger. Anyone could understand that. But Angerman wished it didn't have to be like that—Hunter skirting around him carefully the way he would step around a snake, avoiding his eyes.

Laughter from inside turned Angerman away from watching Hunter stow the gear. In the house, Baby and

Doll were playing some kind of peekaboo-jumping-out-from-behind-the-sofa game with Puppy and Kitty, and the two strays were giggling like real children. Teacher was studying her lumpy scrapbook, and Mommy sat in a chair holding Teddy Bear between her knees, looking into his face and telling him something quietly with a smile. She was reassuring him, probably, comforting his fears. Angerman stood watching them, letting the family-ness of it cup his heart like a little bird.

Then he stepped into the house, and everyone stopped what they were doing to stare at him. Their expressions became wary. When he saw that, when he saw the effect he had on them and how he ruined their happy family routines, he almost turned away. It was the same feeling he had when he saw a bird fly off at his approach: abandonment, left-behindness. Hunter slid past him through the doorway, not touching him, to pick up another load.

A voice, *that voice*, was coming nearer, Bad Guy's voice, saying something cruel and horrible, but Angerman made it stay away. He looked at Mommy and made her meet his gaze. She was the heart of the family.

"I came back to the bridge because—" He pushed that bad whispering voice out of his head. "Because I didn't want to leave you all behind. Not because I can't take care of them." He jerked his chin toward the wild children.

Nobody answered him. Mommy patted Teddy Bear's shoulder, frowning, not really looking away from Angerman but not exactly meeting his eyes either. Action Figure had appeared from the kitchen and now lurked in the doorway of the living room. He held his bow and arrow at the ready, as if he was prepared to use them on

Angerman. Teddy Bear was gripping his alligator stick, too, not as fierce as Action Figure but just as determined. Angerman shifted his gaze to Teacher. She still hadn't said a word to him since last night.

"Your book says you guys need me and I need you. Doesn't it?"

"Maybe." Teacher shrugged, noncommittal and cold. "It's hard to tell."

"It does. I'm sure it does." Angerman appealed to the girls, to Teddy Bear, to the strays. "I don't mean to—to say those scary things I say sometimes. There's this voice, I think it's Bad Guy—and he's the one that hit—"

They were beginning to look frightened again, and Angerman stopped before he said something awful. He glanced around, looking for Bad Guy, sure that devil was trying to get away, make plans to hurt them, set traps for them to fall into. Angerman could feel that rage rising in him, and forced it down. He could not let Bad Guy control him this way.

"I'm sorry. Forget it," he mumbled, turning away and pushing the screen door open.

He stood on the porch for a few moments, staring out at the rain-swollen river. On the opposite bank, a half-submerged bush suddenly swayed and was swept away. Hunter had already rigged up Mommy's tent over the bass boat, and its sides luffed in the breeze like sails. Angerman heard footsteps behind him, and then the squeal of the screen door hinge.

"River's kinda high," Teacher said. She kept her eyes straight ahead. "Do you think it's okay to keep going?"

Relief washed through Angerman. *It was okay. It would be okay.*

"Sure. We don't have to fight against the current—it'll just be faster. And that's a good thing," he said, his voice eager. "We'll get to the ocean faster."

Teacher was nodding, her lips pursed into a thoughtful expression. "Yeah. You're right."

The hinges squeaked again, and Hunter and Action Figure came out. "Come on—let's get those boats loaded," Hunter said.

"Come on, kids," Mommy was saying inside. "Time to go."

Angerman hoisted a box full of camping food into his arms and headed down to the boats. "Let's tie the boats together today, make sure we don't get separated."

By the time they were all loaded—and Baby had gone back to the house once to get a spoon that she liked, and Teddy Bear had climbed out and run into the bushes to have a pee because he was nervous, and Mommy was safely installed in the tent with Puppy and Kitty—the sun was higher and the early breeze had died down. Hunter and Angerman shoved the boats out into the current and they slipped down the river, the house disappearing into the jungle.

The pull of the river was surprisingly strong. The canoe, towed behind the bass boat, kept slewing from side to side and jerking on the tether. Without a keel it was hard for them to maneuver except on quiet water, and the swiftness of the current was making it clumsy. Angerman sat in the stern with his paddle dug into the water, trying to keep the canoe on an even course. Teddy Bear and Baby sat in the middle, between the thwarts, gripping the sides of the canoe. Bad Guy lay facedown on the bottom, where Angerman could keep an eye on him.

He saw Baby's shoulders twitch each time the canoe bumped into a floating branch.

"I don't see no gators, no sir, no gators," Teddy Bear was chanting. He held his alligator stick overhand, for downward jabbing.

"Careful with that stick, Ted," Angerman warned.

"Gotta be ready," Teddy Bear replied. He kept swiveling his head from side to side as he scanned the river for predators.

Ahead, Hunter was struggling with one of the oars, using it to pole the bass boat along instead of rowing. The river was so strong they wanted to see where they were going, instead of sitting the regular way with their backs to the front of the boat. Teacher poled on the riverbank side, fending the boat off submerged stumps and floating logs. A great blue heron lifted itself up from the shallows and flapped off, its long legs trailing behind and dripping water that glinted in the sunlight. Behind them there was a splash—a fish jumping, maybe, or a tree toppling into the water. A turtle scooted to the end of a log on the bank and plopped in. On either side, the overarching trees cast a heavy shade onto the river, with wedges of sunshine cutting through here and there. Angerman felt the pull of the water strengthen.

"The river's getting thinner," Hunter said. His oar stuck in the mud and pushed him off balance, but he wrenched it free. The muck stirred up went swirling ahead of them.

"Shoot, lookout!" Teacher cried out.

There was a *thunk* as the bass boat struck a glancing blow against a cypress stump. They scraped alongside it, and Angerman swung his paddle to that side to push the canoe away. Baby looked back over her shoulder, her eyes wide.

"We're okay," Angerman said.

He heard a muffled laugh from the bottom of the boat, and his blood chilled.

"We're okay," Baby repeated.

There was that laugh again, a little louder. Angerman dug his paddle in, ignoring Bad Guy and his sneering. As the river narrowed the current grew even stronger, forcing the flotilla of debris into a tighter pack, and floating branches scraped and scratched against the canoe and the bigger boat. The flap of the tent opened and Mommy looked out.

"Feels like we're going faster," she said as Puppy and Kitty crawled out past her to stare at the trees racing past. "What's happening?"

Angerman glanced down as his paddle struck something below the water. He could see a submerged log jutting upward; they had just missed hitting it. Then his attention was caught by another loglike shape floating beneath the surface. It rose, and blinked its eyes. Angerman's heart thumped.

Then, when he looked forward again, he saw Hunter and Teacher focused on their oars instead of on the river ahead, and beyond them he saw a large tree fallen sideways across their path and halfway into the middle of the waterway. He jammed his paddle down, trying to brake. "Look out!"

Too late, Hunter and Teacher saw what they were bearing down on, and they both shouted at once, giving different orders. Angerman back-paddled as hard as he could, but the canoe was dragged forward by the bass boat. The bigger boat rammed into the tree, the tent snagging in the branches even as the canoe swung around backward and past in the middle of the river. There was a jerk as the tether ran out of slack. Baby and Teddy Bear both yelped, and Angerman found himself facing upriver. The current dragged hard on the canoe until the dripping tether rope was stretched taut. The snickering in the bottom of the canoe was definitely louder now.

"Can you get unstuck?" Angerman called out.

"Shoot." Teacher was standing up in the boat, trying to unsnag the tent lines and getting her own hair snarled in the branches.

Hunter was leaning on the oar, trying to push the boat away from the tree. The rope tying the two boats together was hooked around a projecting branch, sawing back and forth across the bark as the river pulled at the canoe. "I'm trying," Hunter said, grunting with the effort. "This is crazy, having two boats. We should all be in one."

"Won't it be crowded?" Doll asked.

"Look." Hunter stopped his poling for a moment and shifted his feet. The boat did a sideways dip that brought a loud bark from Puppy. "If we weren't tied together, you guys would already be way ahead, and you might not be able to stop. We'd be separated."

Mommy edged herself outside the tent, giving the situation an apprehensive survey. "Hunter's right. We should all be together."

Teddy Bear was turning from side to side faster and faster, trying to watch for alligators, and the canoe was bouncing and rocking each time he shifted his weight.

"Cut it out, Teddy, my man, don't rock the boat. Okay, then," Angerman agreed. He waited for a moment, and saw Hunter and Teacher and Mommy waiting for him. "You mean, switch right now?"

Teacher nodded. "If we all get into this boat, we can cut the canoe loose and then we can all work to get free of this tree."

Never switch horses in the middle of the stream, Bad Guy said, chuckling. *Haven't you ever heard that rule?*

Angerman slid off his seat and kneeled on Bad Guy, pressing all his weight onto the middle of the mannequin's back to shut him up. "Okay," he said to the others. "Let's get these supplies over. Teddy, Baby, you scoot back this way. I have to get up front where you are so I can get us to the tree."

The two were so taut with fear that it was difficult for Angerman to maneuver past them, and when Baby didn't want to crawl over Bad Guy, Angerman had to reach back and drag the mannequin up into the front of the canoe with him. Bad Guy was giggling away, saying things like *I'm tickled pink, what a lark!* And *This should be fun!* while Angerman pulled hand over hand on the tether rope, dragging the canoe back against the current to the tree.

Hunter leaned out as the canoe came nearer, and then grabbed for the handhold on the bow of the canoe. "I've got it," he said.

Angerman reached for Bad Guy, lifting him up over the gunnels. His stiff plastic legs cracked against the side.

"You can't bring that!" Teacher blurted out. "We're going to be crowded enough already!"

"I'm not leaving him."

Hunter met Angerman's gaze over his outstretched arms. "Can't you take his legs off or something?"

Without a word, Angerman began pulling at the rigid, unjointed legs until they snapped off, smiling with satisfaction at the shriek of pain from Bad Guy. He didn't know why he had never thought of it before—cutting Bad Guy down to size a little bit, making it harder for him to cause trouble. He tossed the legs overboard, where the current spun them away and then pressed them up against another sunken log. They bobbed there, washed over with brown water. Teddy Bear stared in horror at them.

"Here," Angerman said, handing Bad Guy over into the other boat. Torso, arms, and head, that's all the mannequin was now.

"Gator!" Teddy Bear gasped, lunging to his feet. The canoe rocked as Teddy Bear brandished his alligator stick.

"Teddy, sit down!" Teacher yelled.

They all looked where Teddy Bear was pointing with his alligator stick. A long, nubbly brown snout poked at Bad Guy's legs. One of them, freed from being pinned against the log, floated down the river.

Angerman resisted a vengeful laugh and concentrated on handing over the camping gear and food stowed in the canoe. Then he put his hands on either side of the gunnels, making to step out and into the bass boat.

"Hunter has to hold the canoe, and I'll lift you over," he instructed Teddy Bear and Baby. "When I step out of the canoe, you move up here to the front, okay?"

The two nodded. They looked very frightened. Mommy leaned forward, smiling for them. "You'll be fine, kids. Angerman will help you get out."

Angerman reached for the oarlock on the nearside of the bass boat, and prepared to pull himself out of the canoe. As he swung his leg down into the bigger boat, he caught sight of Bad Guy, propped up right behind Puppy and Kitty. "NO!" he shouted, lunging forward.

Startled, Hunter let go of the canoe and swung around. "What the—"

Angerman tackled Bad Guy, throwing him backward away from the strays. "Keep away from them!"

"Mommy!"

"Baby! Teddy!" Mommy cried out, turning away from Angerman with a look of stunned surprise.

The canoe was speeding backward, the tether line snaking out of the bow as the current swept the canoe and the children away. Angerman saw the line go taut, and heard Mommy scream as the frayed rope snapped. Terrified, Baby and Teddy Bear both stood up. The canoe wobbled as it spun around, rammed against another sunken tree stump, and threw Baby into the river, while Bad Guy's hysterical laughter screeched and cackled in Angerman's head.

Baby disappeared under water and then bobbed up again, spluttering and crying as the current pulled her downriver. With a cry, Mommy began clawing at the tent, tearing and ripping it away from the tangle of branches. At the same time, Hunter and Angerman both dove overboard and began swimming toward Teddy Bear and Baby. Teacher began pushing her oar, leaning all her weight against it to shift the boat away from the tree. The little ones were crying—Doll was screaming—and Action Figure was yelling gibberish, jumping up and down in a rage.

Mommy glanced down the river, saw Baby clinging to a low, horizontal branch that hung a couple of feet above the surface. Baby's legs dangled in the water, and the current splashed up around her waist. The girl looked frozen with fear. Mommy turned back to her task, ripping at the stubborn nylon fabric that was holding them captive.

"Oh, no—" Teacher let out a moan. "An alligator!" Then, with a rising scream, "Teddy! TEDDY, NO!"

It was too late. Teddy Bear leaped into the river with his alligator stick. Hunter and Angerman were swimming with hard strokes toward the children, but an alligator was slithering down the muddy bank.

"Hurry!" Mommy shrieked. She began tossing through their gear, desperate for the sharp knife. She found it and began slashing at the tough strings that held the tent onto the boat. One popped loose, then another, and Teacher was shoving with all her might on the oar. Leaves and twigs snapped in their faces.

The bass boat pulled loose from the tent and from the tree, as Teacher shoved and pushed it out into the current. Ahead, they saw Hunter and Angerman push the canoe into the stream again and drag themselves up and into it. They paddled with their hands, reaching and grabbing at the water to speed themselves toward Teddy Bear and Baby.

Both children were now clinging to the branch, water swirling up to their knees. As Hunter and Angerman drove the canoe toward them, the branch snapped and sagged. Baby and Teddy Bear were dunked into the water up to their chins, but they held on.

"Where's the alligator?" Mommy screamed. "Where's the alligator?" The bass boat was bringing them closer and closer, but she couldn't see where the monster had gone.

Hunter made a swipe at the branch and held on, and Angerman leaned out, one hand clutching Baby's shirt and one hand grasping Teddy Bear. He heaved backward, dragging both children into the canoe, flopping them over the sides like wet fish.

At the same time, the bass boat swept into grabbing distance. Hunter switched his hands from the branch to the sides of the bass boat and hung on for dear life as both boats began racing down the river. His palms were gashed and bleeding. Ten feet away, the alligator sank slowly out of view.

"Everyone into this boat," Mommy said, her voice shaking so much she could hardly get the words out.

"Do it fast!" Hunter gasped, straining to keep the boats together as they raced forward.

Teacher reached for Teddy Bear and helped him clamber over and into the boat. "You were so brave, Teddy," Teacher sobbed as she clutched him to her. "You were so brave!"

"You next!" Angerman said to Baby.

She began to scream, terrified as a gap opened between the two boats. "NO! NO!"

"Go on!" Hunter yelled, pulling hard to keep the boats close together.

Mommy leaned out. "You can do it, Baby. Come on!"

Whimpering, Baby reached toward Mommy. Angerman

held on to Baby's other hand while she crawled across, and then he came over, too. He leaned out and held the canoe for Hunter; and for a moment, both boats slowed down as the river split to go around a logjam. When they were all aboard the bass boat, the canoe slid away, dragged into a side current.

Mommy held Baby close, feeling the little girl's body tremble as much as hers was. "Shhhh, you're safe now. You're safe."

Angerman leaned his elbows on his knees while his wet clothes dribbled and dripped. He looked around, noticing the difference in the boat. "Where's the tent?"

"Gone," Mommy mumbled into Baby's hair. "We had to get rid of it."

She hugged Baby even closer, and when she realized no one was speaking, she looked up. Sunlight poured onto her face. She tipped her head back and looked at the narrow band of sky slipping by overhead between the trees. Sky . . .

Mommy looked from Teacher to Hunter to Angerman and quavered a weak smile. "I'm okay. We're all safe. We're going to be . . . just . . . fine."

Chapter Twenty

That night, Teacher had a dream.

In the dream, her name was Virginia. She was wearing a brand-new red dress and white tights that sagged around her knees and black Mary Janes that pinched her toes. Daddy had brushed her hair until it shone. Mother had let her borrow her good pearl necklace.

They were in a big room, a school cafetorium. She was sitting in the front row between Mother and Daddy. Her little brother was on Mother's lap, dressed in a sailor suit and hugging his scruffy brown bear to his chest. Her baby sister was squirming on Daddy's knees, and he was feeding her raisins, trying to keep her still.

Up on the stage, a girl was playing "Für Elise" on the big piano.

Virginia squirmed, too, and tried to still her dancing nerves. G flat major, pianissimo, don't forget—no A-flat in the second measure. She made chords in the air, banged her feet against the rungs of the chair.

"Shhh," someone behind her whispered.

Virginia stopped banging her feet and scrunched up close to Mother. She breathed in the warm vanilla smell of Mother's skin. She stroked the downy curve of Mother's arm.

Mother leaned over and kissed the top of her head. "You're going to do fine, Ginny Bee," she whispered.

There was a burst of applause. "Für Elise" was over, and the girl was standing, taking a bow.

A man in nice Grown-up clothes walked up to the microphone, which let out a squeal of feedback. "Next—" squeal *"will hear Debussy's 'Clair de Lune,' played by Virginia—"* squeal.

Virginia took a deep breath and scraped her sweaty palms across her dress. There was more applause. She started to get up.

Her brother thrust his stuffed bear at her face. "Kiss Teddy first!" he demanded.

Virginia hesitated, then leaned over and kissed its hard black nose. The bear smelled like her brother, all sweetness and sweat.

Her brother giggled, pleased that she had obeyed him. "Teddy wuv Ginny," he said, pointing a stubby finger at her.

It was their game. "And Ginny loves Teddy," she said, kissing the tip of his finger.

She felt Daddy squeeze her hand, heard him whisper, "You're our shining star!" She beamed at him and rose to her feet. And so she walked up to the stage—her mind rehearsing the opening measures of "Clair de Lune" while her heart bloomed like a flower in the warmth of her family's love, in the knowledge that they were all gathered in the cafetorium of Allamanda Elementary School cheering for her, calling out her name. Ginny, Ginny, our Ginny.

She woke up on the crest of her dream, all snug in the cocoon of it. She blinked in confusion: Where was the cafetorium? Where was her family? Instead of applause and Beethoven and Debussy it was twanging bullfrogs, chirping crickets, the grunt of an alligator. And somewhere near her head there were soft little snores, rustling blankets, a small voice murmuring, *"Go to sleep now, Dolly, you have School in the morning."*

Teacher propped herself up on her elbows. Moonlight slanted through the grimy windows and made everything silvery-blue. *Clair de Lune* was "moonlight," she remembered that. Across the floor of the cabin, there were silvery-blue bodies, sleeping bags, pillows. There, near the woodstove, was Mommy spooned around Baby and Doll. There, near the front door, was Angerman curled up in a fetal position. The legless Bad Guy was lying next to him, his head wrapped in fishing net, his wrists bound with one of the girls' dress-up scarves.

Oh, right, Teacher thought. *Oh, right. This.*

Her eyes continued sweeping the room. In the silvery-blue darkness, two bright eyes blinked back at her.

Teddy Bear was awake. He climbed out of his sleeping bag, crawled past a rusty tackle box and around two old fur-covered dog beds containing Puppy and Kitty, and sat down at Teacher's feet.

Teacher hoisted herself up so they were face-to-face. "What's the matter—can't sleep?" she whispered.

Teddy Bear shook his head. "No, uh-uh, can't sleep."

Teacher put her hands on his thin shoulders. "You went through a lot today," she reminded him. And then she noticed his expression. "What is it, Teddy? What?"

The little boy blinked at her. "Last time, alligator got her," he whispered. "He *got* her."

Teacher tried to keep her hands steady on his shoulders, even as she bit back a cry. "I know, Teddy."

"Couldn't stop him," Teddy Bear whispered.

"It's okay—she's with Mother and Daddy in heaven," Teacher told him in a quivering voice.

The two of them glanced up. There was a gaping hole in the roof of the cabin. Through it, they could see the black sky, a sprinkling of stars, the white curve of the moon.

"Do you 'member her name?" Teddy Bear asked her.

Teacher felt tears stinging her eyes. "No. Do you?"

Teddy Bear shook his head. "Do you 'member what she looked like?"

Teacher searched the cobwebby haze of her brain, scoured for memories, bits of her dream. Nothing came to her. "No, uh-uh."

"Me neither."

Teacher and Teddy Bear stared at each other. *My brother, he's my brother—how could I forget that?* she thought as she felt him crawling into her lap, snuggling against her chest. She wrapped her arms around him as tight as she could, then picked up one of his hands and kissed a single fingertip. "It's okay, shhh, Teddy, it's okay. From now on we have each other, we can help each other try to remember."

On the seventh day, they reached a big city. As Angerman pulled the oar through the brackish water he looked up at the tall gray glass-and-steel buildings that loomed over them. Some of the buildings had words on their sides, words like *Mutual, Trust, Corporation, Inc.* He wondered where on earth they were. How much farther did this river go?

"Whassat, whassat?" Action Figure cried out from the back of the bass boat. He was pointing to the riverbank, where three strange-looking birds as tall as Grown-ups were loping past the St. John's Crisis Care Center and the El Loco Taco House.

"Ostriches," Angerman replied.

"How'd you know that, Angerman?" Hunter asked him. He was pulling the oar on the other side of the boat.

"Dunno, just do. They're not wild birds, though. Must've been a zoo around here at one time. They must've escaped."

"The name of this ancient city is Jacksonville," Teacher announced. "So says The Book." She was sitting in the middle of the boat between Mommy and Teddy Bear, poring over her crazy scrapbook. "We're near the ocean."

"What's ocean?" Doll asked. She and the other little ones were picking through the luggage, playing with toothbrushes and thermoses and bungee cords.

"It's a large body of salt water," Teacher explained. "It will help guide us to Washington, our ultimate destination. Smell the water, now? The ocean salt reaches into the river. That's how you know we're close."

Mommy glanced around. Mangroves had begun colonizing a flooded car dealership. Faded plastic penants were tangled among the shrubby tentacles. "It's so weird, with no people," she murmured. "We're the only ones in this ancient city."

"We're the only ones anywhere," Hunter pointed out to her. "Angerman, paddle a little faster, wouldja?"

"I can relieve you if you're tired, Angerman," Mommy offered. "I'll take a turn."

Angerman swiped the sweat off his forehead with the

bottom of his T-shirt and plunged his oar into the river. Water splashed over the side of the boat and got Puppy and Kitty in the face. They giggled and shrieked.

Arise and be baptized.

"Sorry, guys," Angerman apologized. "I'm okay for now, thanks, Mommy."

For the past few days he had concentrated on being part of the family, being Real Normal, even though Bad Guy had been whispering to him more and more, especially at night when all the others were asleep. He didn't want them all to know, however, or let them think he wasn't just a regular kid like they were, so he had kept his mouth shut, had kept to himself. Had kept his hands off Bad Guy and the picture frame whenever the strangeness overtook him. Even if it meant asking Action Figure to hide them from him, or even tie his wrists with rope. It was worth it, to keep everyone wanting him in the family.

The river had forked and spread out across a highway, where cars stood up to their hoods in water. An anhinga sat on a pickup truck roof, holding its wings out to dry. They were approaching a large concrete-and-steel bridge. The sign on it read FULLER WARREN BRIDGE. Some bird had made a nest under one of the trestles. Angerman could see the tiny brown heads, the upturned gaping mouths.

"Whassat?" Action Figure pointed.

"Birds," Angerman replied. "Waiting for their mommy to bring them lunch."

"No, whassat next to birds?" Action Figure asked him.

Angerman squinted. Someone had spray-painted an

image onto the bridge, to the right of the birds' nest. It was silvery-gray against the shiny black enamel of the trestle.

"It's a horsey," Teddy Bear spoke up. "It's a picture of a gray horsey!"

From under a pile of sleeping bags, Bad Guy began to cackle.

A pale horse.

Angerman felt bile rise in his throat, felt a wave of dizziness overcome him. He gripped his oar tighter, leaned his chest against it.

Well, isn't THAT a horse of a different color? Bad Guy snickered.

"Shut up!" Angerman hissed under his breath.

Ever hear of a dark horse candidate for president?

Angerman closed his eyes and willed the dizziness to go away. But from out of nowhere, images began flashing through his mind.

A chariot.

A long black car with men in suits jogging beside it.

A sword.

A big window overlooking the ocean.

And then a voice, not Bad Guy's, came to him. *And I looked, and behold a pale horse: and his name that sat on him was Death, and Hell followed with him.*

"We're all gonna die," Angerman whispered.

"What?"

Angerman's eyes flew open. Mommy was staring at him with a strange expression on her face. "Did you say something?"

Angerman shook his head. "No, no, it's nothing."

"You all right?"

"Fine."

Didn't know horses liked to eat dogs and cats, did you, boy? Bad Guy cackled.

Making sure no one was looking, Angerman stepped on Bad Guy through the pile of sleeping bags and ground his heel. "Shut up, I told you, shut up," he hissed.

"You *sure* you're all right? You look all pale," Mommy persisted.

"I'm fine, I told you."

Angerman turned away from Mommy and stared up at the bridge and felt the lie sitting heavy on his heart.

He knew the horse was a sign. He knew something terrible had begun.

The sun was low in the sky when they reached the mouth of the river. Mommy felt the breeze in her hair, tasted the salt on her lips. Behind her, the little ones were chanting, "Ocean, ocean, ocean!" She wanted to stop rowing and sit up in the bass boat, wanted to see what lay beyond the endless field of murky seagrass. But she made herself be patient. They would be there soon enough.

"Anyone remember the beach?" Hunter called out.

"Dolly's been to the beach," Doll spoke up. "She said she ate bugs there and stuff."

"No, uh-uh, you don't eat bugs on the beach—you eat clambakes and sunscreen," Baby corrected her. "Teacher learned us that in School."

"Look!"

Teacher was pointing at a ribbon of blue that shimmered along the horizon. "There it is!"

Mommy clapped her hand over her mouth to keep from crying out. The ocean, they had made it to the ocean. She started to row faster, and so did Teacher. The prow of the bass boat cut smoothly through the field of grass and made it part. Flamingos rose in a cloud of flashing pink, filling the sky.

Soon the ribbon of blue became wider. Seagulls swooped through the air with shrill cries, and egrets plucked their way through the brackish water. Patches of sand, dotted with tiny seashells and strange dead sea creatures, began to replace the field of grass.

"There's the beach!" Hunter cried. "Paddle to the bank—let's get out."

"Ya-ya!" Action Figure cried.

Mommy and Teacher pointed the bass boat toward the bank. Hunter rolled up his pants, jumped out, and guided the boat onto the sand. Action Figure bounded out of the boat to help his brother, and was immediately soaked from head to toe. He stomped through the water, whooping and hollering and splashing.

As soon as the boat was on land, everyone else leaped out, too. Mommy rolled up her jeans and felt her bare feet touch the smooth sand. She followed the others, who were running toward the shore.

It seemed like a miracle to her that they were here. That she was at the beach with the sun warm on her face, with the wind tossing her hair, with her children racing around, giddy as monkeys and singing happy ocean songs.

"We did it! We made it!" Hunter shouted as he ran into a crashing wave and was knocked down. He hoisted himself up, laughing and sputtering.

Teacher had stopped at the edge of the sand and was

staring out at the waves. Mommy stopped next to her, trying to catch her breath. "Look, dolphins!" she said, pointing. Twenty yards out, sleek gray backs wheeled up and down through the surf. As the girls watched, one dolphin shot out of the water. Mommy reached for Teacher's hand and squeezed. Her heart was full. "Keep America Beautiful," she whispered.

"Let's pick up some driftwood and make a fire," Teacher suggested. "A real bonfire, like it was done in the Before Time."

"I remember going to the beach," Mommy said. "With—with my First Family."

"What d'you remember about it?" Teacher asked her in a gentle voice.

Mommy shook her head. "Nothing, you know, *specific*. I remember I was happy."

Teacher smiled. "That's a good memory, then."

The sun was setting behind them, and the sky over the ocean was aflame with color. Small stilt-legged birds ran back and forth on the wet sand, retreating from the breaking waves and then rushing down again, jabbing into the sand for dinner. While the little kids splashed around in the water, Mommy, Teacher, and Hunter began collecting driftwood. Angerman went to the bass boat to retrieve their gear. When there was enough wood, Mommy got the camping matches and lit the tiny scraps of kindling.

The kindling hissed and spit as the flames caught. Then the fire started to burn in earnest. Angerman, Mommy, Teacher, and Hunter hunkered down in a semicircle around it and rubbed their hands against its warmth. Mommy wrapped her arms around herself and moved closer to the fire. Night was coming, and the air was growing cool.

Just then, Angerman began rifling through their gear, tossing things aside in an urgent search. "What're you looking for?" Hunter asked him.

Angerman got his picture frame out of one of the bags and lifted it to his face. "Good evening!" he said. "And now, a special news bulletin!"

Mommy frowned. Not *again*. "Angerman," she warned.

"This just in! There's a Grown-up on the beach," Angerman announced.

Mommy whirled around. Near the rocks, near where the children were splashing and playing, there was a woman dressed all in white.

Standing there.

Watching them.